HARLEQUIN® Presents

Welcome to the new collection of Harlequin Presents!

Don't miss contributions from favorite authors Michelle Reid, Kim Lawrence and Susan Napier, as well as the second part of Jane Porter's THE DESERT KINGS series, Lucy Gordon's passionate Italian, Chantelle Shaw's Tuscan tycoon and Jennie Lucas's sexy Spaniard! And look out for Trish Wylie's brilliant debut Presents book, *Her Bedroom Surrender!*

We'd love to hear what you think about Harlequin Presents. E-mail us at Presents@hmb.co.uk or join in the discussions at www.iheartpresents.com and www.sensationalromance.blogspot.com, where you'll also find more information about books and authors!

INNOCENT MISTRESS, VIRGIN BRIDE

Wedded and bedded for the very first time!

Classic romances from your favorite
Harlequin Presents authors

Available this month:

The Spaniard's Defiant Virgin
by Jennie Lucas

Only in Harlequin Presents®

Jennie Lucas

THE SPANIARD'S DEFIANT VIRGIN

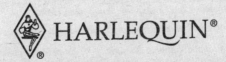

INNOCENT MISTRESS,
VIRGIN BRIDE

HARLEQUIN®

TORONTO • NEW YORK • LONDON
AMSTERDAM • PARIS • SYDNEY • HAMBURG
STOCKHOLM • ATHENS • TOKYO • MILAN • MADRID
PRAGUE • WARSAW • BUDAPEST • AUCKLAND

ISBN-13: 978-0-373-12728-3
ISBN-10:   0-373-12728-6

THE SPANIARD'S DEFIANT VIRGIN

First North American Publication 2008.

Copyright © 2007 by Jennie Lucas.

All about the author...
Jennie Lucas

JENNIE LUCAS had a tragic beginning for any would-be writer: a very happy childhood. Her parents owned a bookstore, and she grew up surrounded by books, dreaming about faraway lands. When she was ten, her father secretly paid her a dollar for every classic novel (*Jane Eyre, War and Peace*) that she read.

At fifteen, she went to a Connecticut boarding school on scholarship. She took her first solo trip to Europe at sixteen, then put off college and traveled around the U.S., supporting herself with jobs as diverse as gas-station cashier and newspaper advertising assistant.

At twenty-two, she met the man who would be her husband. For the first time in her life, she wanted to stay in one place, as long as she could be with him. After their marriage, she graduated from Kent State University with a degree in English, and started writing books a year later.

Jennie was a finalist in the Romance Writers of America's Golden Heart contest in 2003, and won the award in 2005. A fellow 2003 finalist, Australian author Trish Morey, read Jennie's writing and told her that she should write for Harlequin Presents. It seemed like too big a dream, but Jennie took a deep breath and went for it. A year later, Jennie got the magical call from London that turned her into a published author.

Since then, life has been hectic—juggling a writing career, a sexy husband and two young children—but Jennie loves her crazy, chaotic life. Now if she can only figure out how to pack up her family and live in all the places she's writing about!

For more about Jennie and her books, please visit her Web site at www.jennielucas.com.

To my husband, who is better than ice cream.

CHAPTER ONE

Tarfaya, Morocco

HE WAS waiting for her outside the Dar el-Saladin.

Marcos Ramirez held up his binoculars, watching the flower-covered limousine leave the fishing village in a whirlwind of rose petals. From where Marcos stood, the sturdy gate that protected the village from sandstorms on one side and the sea on the other seemed riddled with red bullet holes.

Tamsin Winter, at last. He'd kept tabs on her through her ten cloistered years in boarding schools until she'd returned to London last year. Since then, the wild young heiress had frequently been in the tabloids, always with a different man on her arm. The spoiled beauty was reputedly the most accomplished flirt in Britain.

Breaking her would be a pleasure.

"The car's moving into position, *Patrón*," his chief bodyguard, Reyes, noted aloud.

"*Sí*." Marcos put down the binoculars. He knew his men could have kidnapped the Winter girl without his supervision, preventing her from arriving at her wedding in the Sheikh's kasbah to the north. Marcos could be taking his ease in Madrid right now, drinking coffee and checking the latest numbers on the London and New York stock exchanges instead of sweating in the dust-choked desert.

But he'd been dreaming of revenge for twenty years, and today was the culmination of everything. After he had the girl, both she and her family would be utterly destroyed. Finally. As they deserved.

Marcos smiled grimly to himself. He only wished he could see the expression on her bridegroom's face when he heard the news, the black-hearted bastard.

The limousine left the village, moving along the sand-covered road that separated the Sahara and the bright Atlantic shore. He pulled his black mask down over his face and turned to Reyes. *"Vámonos."*

Tamsin Winter had just sold her virginity to the highest bidder.

Her white bridal kaftan, intricately embroidered with silver thread and jewels, weighed on her like a shroud as she looked through the darkened windows. She felt almost envious of a wrinkled woman selling oranges on the street. Selling oranges seemed like a pleasant fate compared with marrying a man who'd already beaten one wife to death.

She took a deep breath, closing her eyes. It didn't matter, she told herself. She would let Aziz al-Maghrib paw at her with his meaty hands, kiss her with the stench of his foul breath and take her innocence with his flabby, wrinkled body. It would be a small price to pay, since it would save her young sister from a life of misery and neglect.

But, as recently as last month, she'd looked forward to falling in love and marrying a man she could cherish. She'd dreamed of starting a career and some day having children of her own. She'd spent all of her twenty-three years dreaming of the day her life would truly begin.

Strange to think that it was already over.

Saving her sister was the best choice she'd ever made. But, even knowing that, part of her ached for all the time she'd wasted, the romances she'd never had, the chances she'd never taken. If she'd known her life would be so short...

"Tamsin! Stop fidgeting. You'll wrinkle your dress. Oh, you're doing it on purpose, you stupid girl!"

Tamsin slowly opened her eyes, heavy with black kohl, and looked into the hated face of her half-brother's wife. Camilla Winter was twenty years older than Tamsin, and her surgery-smoothed skin stretched oddly over her skull.

"Did you pay for your face-lift out of Nicole's money, Camilla?" Tamsin asked curiously. "Is that why you were letting a ten-year-old girl starve? So you could look like a doll?"

Camilla gasped.

"Do not fear. My brother will beat the rebellious spirit out of her," Hatima, her future sister-in-law, said confidently. Hatima and Camilla comprised her *negaffa*—the older female relatives who, according to Moroccan tradition, were supposed to help a young bride, to counsel her, to calm her fears about her coming marriage.

Some help, Tamsin thought bitterly. She looked down at her henna-decorated hands folded carefully in her lap. But Hatima was right. Her husband would beat her, either before or after he took her virginity. Maybe both.

She stared out the window as they passed the gate that encircled the village. She never should have saved herself for love, she thought. She should have slept with the first boy who'd drunkenly kissed her at a college party. Then maybe it wouldn't hurt so much now.

"What? No snappy comeback?" Camilla sneered. "Not so brave now, are you?"

Blinking hard to hold back the tears—she'd die before she cried in front of Camilla—Tamsin stared stonily at the fishing boats bobbing off the shore and the seagulls flying free over the ocean. Seemingly disappointed by her lack of spirit, the other women began to speak of recent attacks in nearby Laayoune.

"The *wali*'s wife was kidnapped," Hatima whispered. "Taken in broad daylight."

"What's the world coming to?" Camilla replied gleefully. "What happened to her?"

Traffic waned as they traveled northwards along the Atlantic, but the car weaved back and forth across the road. Frowning, Tamsin glanced up at the driver. Though the car was cold with air-conditioning, the back of his neck was covered with sweat.

"The *wali* had to sell everything he owned to pay the ransom. The family is ruined, of course, but at least the wife was returned."

"You mean they didn't hurt her?" Camilla sounded disappointed.

"No, they just wanted money. It was—"

Hatima's voice ended in a scream as their driver

veered hard right and slammed on the brakes. The limousine spun around twice, skidding across the road before it crashed heavily into a sandbank.

The driver threw open his door and ran back towards Tarfaya.

"Where are you going?" Camilla cried. Her long nails scraped against the handle as she reached for her door.

The door handle was abruptly yanked out of her hand from the other side. Three men in black masks and desert camouflage leaned threateningly into the back seat, shouting orders in a language that Tamsin didn't understand.

Her own side door was yanked open. She whirled around with a gasp.

A man, taller than the others, towered over her. Beneath his black mask, she could see a cruel mouth and steel-gray eyes that bored into her like a revolver pressing into her flesh.

"Tamsin Winter," he said in English. "At last you are mine."

He knew her name. A strange sort of bandit, she thought dimly, even as she heard the other women screaming behind her. Why would a desert bandit know her name?

Had her prayers been answered and he'd come to save her?

No! she thought desperately. No one could save her. Tamsin had to marry Aziz or her sister would pay the price.

What had Hatima said the bandits wanted? Money? Licking her lips nervously, she sat up straight, trying to stare him down.

"I am the future bride of Aziz ibn Mohamed al-Maghrib," she said. "Touch a hair on my head and he will kill you. Return me safely, and you will be rewarded."

"Ah." The man's mouth stretched into a smile, showing white, even teeth. "And how would he reward me?"

He had a strange accent, the flat vowels of an American punctuated with something more exotic—the rolling Rs of a Spaniard. Who was this man? He was more than a mere brigand. The thought frightened her.

"A million euros," she said recklessly.

"A fine number."

"You'll be rich," she agreed, praying that Aziz's uncle, who held the wealth in the family, would actually pay it.

"A generous offer," the brigand said. "But, unfortunately for you, money is not what I'm after."

He reached into the back seat, grabbing her shoulders. Tamsin screamed, kicking and clawing at his face.

"Don't fight me," he growled.

She only screamed and kicked harder. One of her shoes slammed hard against his groin. Cursing, he restrained her wrists with one hand. Reaching into his pocket, he pulled out a white cloth and pressed it against her mouth.

He was drugging her! She tried not to breathe, but after a minute she couldn't stop herself from taking a gasping breath. The air tasted sickly sweet through the cloth. She tried to twist her face away, but the man wouldn't allow it. She took another breath, and the desert horizon started to spin before it all went black.

* * *

Tamsin woke up in a very soft bed.

She opened her eyes slowly. Her head pounded. She could hear the lapping of water, the creaking of wood, the caw of seagulls overhead.

And she realized she was naked.

Sitting up straight in bed, she pulled the luxurious cotton sheets away from her body. She was wearing her see-through white lace bra and panties—her wedding-night lingerie—and nothing else.

"I trust you slept well."

She yanked the sheets up to her chin. A handsome stranger was leaning against the doorway. He was tall, broad-shouldered and olive-skinned, with short, wavy dark hair. He wore a crisp white shirt and dark pants that molded to his muscular body.

She'd never seen him before, but she recognized his voice. That cruel, sensual mouth. Most of all, those dark, cold eyes.

"Where am I?" She had a hazy memory of being on a helicopter and then driven through the streets of Tangiers. "What did you do with Camilla and Hatima?"

He stepped into the cabin, his gray eyes alight with malignant hatred as he looked at her. "You should be worried about what I'm going to do with you."

That was exactly what she was trying *not* to think about. If she did, she'd start screaming with terror and fear. Not just for herself but for ten-year-old Nicole, who was still held hostage in Tarfaya, depending on her to get through this.

She had to hold herself together long enough to come up with a plan of escape.

"Did you kidnap them as well?" she asked, despising the involuntary tremble in her voice. "Where have you taken me? Have you sent a ransom note to the Sheikh?"

He folded his arms. "There will be no ransom note."

"What?"

He took a step closer to the bed. His whole body was muscular and taut beneath his fine clothes, as if only sheer will kept him from grabbing her.

"I left the others in Tarfaya," he said. "I only need you."

She swallowed. "Me? Why?"

He just stared down at her, his face a handsome, arrogant mask.

She tried again. "Where are we?"

His full, sensual lip curled into a line of contempt. "My yacht."

Well, yes, even she could have guessed that much. She glanced through the port window. The sun was just starting to set, trailing a pathway of crimson and orange across the water. She couldn't see a trace of land. They were out on the open sea, she thought, where no one would hear her scream.

If he hadn't kidnapped her for ransom, then why? No matter what the tabloids seemed to believe, nothing about her was special. And her family had nothing he could want. Her brother's company was hanging on by a thread.

"Who are you?" she whispered.

"Your captor. That's all you need to know."

Tasmin pressed her shaking hands against the sheet to hide their tremor. She couldn't let him see her fear. Bullies lived to control, to inspire terror. She'd learned that from her father. The only way to survive was to respond with defiance. "What do you want with me?"

He sat on the edge of the bed and reached to caress her cheek. "You are a beautiful woman, *señorita*, famed for your power over men. Can't you guess what I want?"

She shivered at his brief touch. Up close, he was even more handsome. Dark and dangerous, he emanated power. If they'd met at a London club, she would have been attracted to him, fascinated even.

Could she really fight a man like this and hope to win?

Her fingers clutched the sheet between them like a shield. *Nicole*, she thought. *Remember Nicole*.

She'd found her little sister alone last month in their brother's cold, darkened Yorkshire mansion, left without food or money while Sheldon and Camilla used her money to support their jet-setting lifestyle. Tamsin still felt a chill of horror when she remembered stepping into the dark house, calling her sister's name; Nicole had run to her crying and flung her thin, shivering body against her. She'd believed that Tamsin had abandoned her.

She would never forgive their half-brother for that. God, she hated Sheldon, she hated Camilla, she despised everyone who hurt innocent, helpless people in pursuit of their own selfish desires.

Like the man in front of her now. She narrowed her eyes. She wouldn't let him prevent her marriage to Aziz.

"If you're going to have me, get it over with," she said

flatly. "And take me back to Morocco so I can be married."

His eyes widened and she saw that she'd surprised him. But, almost as quickly as the expression had appeared, it was gone. He stood up, looking as cold and unreachable as the stars. "I can see why you're known as a flirt."

"Forgive me if I don't know the proper etiquette when I'm kidnapped on my wedding day and wake up naked on a stranger's yacht."

"You're not naked."

"How do you know? Are you the one who undressed me?"

He lifted a sardonic eyebrow. "Alas, I haven't had that pleasure," he said but, before she could relax and be grateful for that small blessing, he added darkly, "yet."

The look he gave her could have melted stone. It was full of hatred, yes, but something more. She felt it simmering through her body, a strange electricity humming through her veins. She found herself staring at his lips. Wondering what he looked like beneath the shirt. Wondering how it would feel to have his body pressed against her own.

She shook the thought away. The only thing that mattered now was finding out what he wanted with her so she could get away. She had to protect Nicole.

Especially since what had happened was Tamsin's fault. It was true they'd never been close—Tamsin had been sent to an American boarding school when her sister was a baby. Their mother had died when they were young, and their father a few years later. But

Tamsin never should have trusted Sheldon to be Nicole's guardian. Never. And while she'd been in London enjoying her first taste of freedom, Sheldon had been ransacking both sisters' trust funds. He'd fired Nicole's nanny, leaving her alone.

Tamsin should have known. She should have protected her…

"We're almost there." Her handsome, arrogant captor moved across the cabin towards the window.

"Where?"

"Andalusia. My home."

Spain! A burst of hope went through Tamsin. Spain meant land beneath her feet, civilization—and freedom! She could catch a high-speed ferry from Algeciras and be back in Morocco by nightfall.

The man turned back abruptly to face her and she lowered her eyes, afraid that he would see her plans written across her face. "Tell me, Señorita Winter, do you speak Spanish?"

"No, I don't," she lied, trying to keep all emotion from her voice. "Do you?"

"Of course." He gave her a smile that wasn't a smile at all. "But my mother was American. I lived in Boston for six years after she died. I will speak English for your sake."

"Then explain to me, in English, why you've kidnapped me."

"Missing your fiancé already?" he asked coldly.

Caught off guard, she stammered, "No…that is to say, yes." She took a breath. "Whether I miss him is beside the point. I made a promise to marry him, so I must. Some people," she said succinctly, "have honor."

His eyes flashed, but were quickly veiled. "So you admit you do not love him."

"I never said that."

"No, you did not, but Aziz al-Maghrib has a reputation for cruelty." His dark gaze skimmed over her, making her wonder if he could somehow see her naked body beneath the sheet. "Are you so shallow that his uncle's wealth makes you wish to be his bride?"

She had no intention of discussing her reasons for the marriage. "If you know Aziz's reputation and you still kidnapped me, you're a fool. He will kill you for this."

He sat on the bed. Close. Too close. She wanted to move away, but his weight held down most of the sheet and what was left was barely enough for modesty. She'd never let any man see her in knickers and a bra and she wasn't going to start now. Especially when just having him close was causing such strange reactions in her own body.

She opened her mouth to demand that he move away. But their eyes met and his gaze was dark, so dark. And full of such emotion that it was an ocean to drown in.

To call him handsome wasn't nearly enough, she thought. His face was breathtaking in its sinister beauty, with his Roman nose, high cheekbones and sharp jaw line. His dark gray eyes contrasted with olive skin and black wavy hair that was just long enough for her to run her hands through, if she'd dared. He was so tall that, even sitting next to her on the bed, she had to look up; he was so broad-shouldered and muscular that she knew he could easily overpower her. He could do anything he wished with her. The thought frightened her.

He reached his hand towards her. She braced for a hit but, to her surprise, he just stroked her cheek.

"I've waited a long time for this." His touch was possessive, gentle, as if she were a wild horse to be tamed to his command. "A lifetime."

"For what?" she managed.

"For you."

"For me?" She almost wished that he would hit her. She would have known how to deal with that. Instead, she was trembling beneath his touch. He didn't even need brute force. Just the brush of his fingers was enough to make her agree to anything he asked, and he was only touching her cheek. What would happen if he stroked her breast, kissed her mouth, pulled her down beneath him on the bed...?

She wrenched her face away. "Why did you kidnap me? What are you going to do to me?"

"You're the spoils of war, Tamsin." He leaned forward to whisper in her ear, "And I want to find out if revenge tastes sweet..."

As he spoke, his lips brushed against the sensitive flesh of her ear. His breath was hot against her neck, causing prickles to run the length of her body.

"Please," she whispered, hardly knowing what she was asking for. Her body felt so strange. Tense and tingly, cold and hot.

He ran his hand down her cheek, past the sensitive flesh of her ear, down her neck. He stroked her hair as he gently pulled back her head, exposing her vulnerable throat, her aching mouth. Involuntarily, she licked her lips. For a suspended instant, his eyes followed the movement of her tongue.

Then his mouth was on hers.

His kiss was hungry, demanding. His tongue stroked inside her mouth, intertwining with hers, teasing her. Longing set her whole body aflame and she wrapped her arms around his broad shoulders. She ran her hands through his dark hair as he deepened the kiss.

"The pictures didn't do you justice," he whispered against her cheek when he drew away. "Men start wars over women like you..."

The hair of his arms brushed against the bare skin of her torso and she looked down with a gasp. The sheet had fallen from her hands and was now crumpled around her waist. His eyes roved over her breasts, her belly, the aroused nipples pushing through the translucent white lace of her bra.

Before she could pull up the sheet, his hands were on her naked skin, grasping her waist as he pulled her roughly against his body.

She didn't fight him. She couldn't. He kissed her, his large hands massaging the bare warmth of her back, and all she could think was that she'd never been kissed like this before. She was lost—lost in him—and the whole world seemed to spin around her as if they were at the center of a whirlwind.

Without thinking, she reached beneath his shirt to imitate the way he touched her, caressing his flat belly, moving her fingertips up his muscular chest. A groan escaped him as he touched her bra clasp.

A hard knock sounded at the door.

He wrenched away. Breathing hard, the two of them stared at each other. He looked dazed, she thought, but not nearly so dazed as she felt.

His expression suddenly changed.

"You're good," he said, and his voice was an accusation.

She was good? As if she were the one who'd been seducing *him*?

He crossed to the door. A young woman waited outside with her arms full. "The clothes for the *señorita*, *Patrón*," she said in Spanish, and left.

Turning back to Tamsin, he tossed a black dress and high-heeled shoes on the bed. "Here. Maria took off your kaftan so you'd be comfortable in bed." His voice was almost a sneer. "These clothes should suit you."

"Y-you're leaving?" she stammered. Her defiance had been burned away in his searing kiss. She could hardly imagine standing, let alone walking, with her knees so weak.

He stared at her for a moment, his face angry and brooding. Then, without answer, he turned back towards the door.

"Wait," she said in a low voice. The day had been a roller coaster of emotion and exhaustion. Tears filled her eyes, threatening to spill over her lashes. "Is that all you have to say to me? You've dragged me from my wedding, kidnapped me across the Mediterranean, kissed me, and now you're going to leave without a single word of explanation?"

His dark eyes narrowed. Dislike emanated from his body like waves of heat in the desert.

"Very well. I will give you that much," he said. "What did you ask? My name? Marcos Ramirez. What do I want with you? It's simple, Miss Winter. I intend to destroy your fiancé and your family, and you're going to help me do it."

CHAPTER TWO

MAYBE he should have let Reyes kidnap the girl after all.

Marcos glanced at the girl sitting next to him in the Rolls-Royce as the chauffeur drove them three miles inland from the coast.

Silent at last. It was an improvement from the previous few hours, when she'd demanded for him to let her go so she could rush back and marry Aziz al-Maghrib. When her demands hadn't worked, she'd tried insults and threats. Thinking about it now almost made him laugh. He was not one of her suitors. Her moods held no sway over him.

Or did they? An image of their kiss flooded his mind. He hadn't meant to kiss her in the cabin of his yacht, but she'd just looked so damned desirable. And the kiss itself…

He pushed the disturbing memory from his mind. The woman was an experienced coquette. According to the tabloids, she'd slept with every male celebrity who set foot in the London boroughs; of course she knew how to kiss. It changed nothing. If anything, it only lowered his opinion of her. Her pretense of bewildered innocence, the way she'd blushed after pretending to drop the sheet—was there anything the woman wouldn't do in order to return to Morocco and get her claws into the al-Maghrib fortune?

He'd actually told her the truth about his plan to destroy her family, but she hadn't asked a word about it. Apparently, her whole family could starve, so long as she herself was slathered with diamonds and rubies as the honored wife of the Sheikh's nephew.

Shallow-hearted and greedy, he thought contemptuously. As venal as her bridegroom, and probably as brainless as her half-brother into the bargain.

A pity she was also the most beautiful woman he'd ever seen.

Her beauty wasn't just in her porcelain skin, her pink lips or her wide blue eyes. It was more than that. Her charm was in the way she moved, like a flamenco dancer. It was in the way her long red hair swayed gracefully against her pale shoulders. It was in the sound of her voice, deep and melodic. It was in her slender, reed-like waist, long legs and full, high breasts. Put all of that together, and he could see why she'd been called the most desirable woman in Britain. A lesser man would instantly be a slave to her charm.

It would serve her right to seduce her, he thought suddenly, glancing at her. She was pressed against the opposite side of his car, glaring at the passing Spanish countryside. How he would love to break her will. To make her sigh and scream with pleasure. To overwhelm her rudeness and insults with an onslaught of desire. His whole body tightened as he thought of it. It would serve the spoiled girl right...

Damn it to hell. He clenched his jaw, realizing that his attraction to her was in danger of overriding his reason. Obviously he was just as susceptible to her charm as any other man. It infuriated him. He had no doubt that he could resist her, but that he'd even thought of taking her to bed proved how dangerous she was.

As the car pulled to the castle's front steps, his gaze unwillingly followed the curves of her body in the low-cut black dress. The Andalusian summer night was sultry and fragrant with jasmine as, with a dismissive motion to the chauffeur, Marcos walked around to her door.

She continued to ignore him. Without a word, he grabbed her arm and pulled her from the car. He dragged her up the wide steps, followed by Reyes, Maria and the others from the van.

She stumbled on the top step, looking up at the crenellated battlements of the fourteenth-century castle. "This is your home?"

"Yes," he said shortly. "And your home for the next few weeks."

Her face shut down in that rebellious expression he knew so well. "I won't stay here. You can't make me."

In spite of everything, he could feel himself starting to lose his patience. Between her beauty and her insolence, she seemed to know just how to get under his skin. "You're here as long as I want you."

She yanked away from him, folding her arms over her deliciously full breasts as she entered the castle. He let her go, confident that she could not escape with the tall, heavy doors closed behind them. The reluctant clack-clack-clack of her high heels echoed against the walls as she followed him, staring upward in amazement. Long ago, the magnificent foyer had been built to impress, with high ceilings carved in intricate designs of flowers, Arabic letters and geometric patterns.

He remembered she'd briefly majored in medieval studies before switching to economics. Hopefully the foyer was impressing her, he thought grimly. She wasn't in London any more. It was time she realized who was in power here.

Holding her prisoner here would financially decimate both of his enemies. Without the wedding between the two families, Sheikh Mohamed ibn Battuta al-Maghrib would not sell the argan oil harvest on credit to Sheldon Winter, which he needed for the relaunch of his only profitable product. The board members of Winter International would sell the company off for parts, and Sheldon would be swamped beneath the weight of his personal debts.

Aziz would be hurt even worse. Without his uncle's promised wedding gift, he would no longer be able to hide his gambling addiction. The Sheikh, an honorable but strict man, would likely disinherit him, and his creditors would break both his legs. A perfect end, in Marcos's opinion.

The only thing that might be even more satisfying would be if Aziz came to Spain to start a war over Tamsin. After what the man had done to his father, nothing would give Marcos more pleasure than to rip him apart with his bare hands. He was sick of secrets. Sick of lies. And, most of all, sick of waiting. He wanted the men who'd destroyed his family punished.

In the meantime, he was stuck with Tamsin Winter as his prisoner.

His eyes traced the outline of her gorgeous figure and the red hair tumbling down her bare back. Her skin was as creamy-pale as winter and looked as soft as a summer breeze. His hands longed to stroke her back, to see if she was as soft as she looked, to see if the fire of her hair was reflected in the tumultuous passion of her embrace.

He shook himself in annoyance. She was his prisoner, he told himself, nothing more. Setting his jaw, he looked at her coldly. "You will join me for dinner tonight."

Her full pink lip curled. "I'd rather starve."

"As you wish." With a flare of his nostril, he turned to his head of security standing discreetly behind them. "Reyes, lock Miss Winter in the tower."

"No!" Her eyes went wide and she took a step towards him. "You can't lock me up!"

"I can and I will." The room he'd prepared for her was luxurious and comfortable, and far from the tower, but he had no intention of sharing that with her. Not after all she'd put him through today. "You've given me no reason to seek your company."

Her hands clenched as she visibly struggled to contain her anger. Her cheeks were red with the effort.

"I've changed my mind," she said through gritted teeth. "I would love to have dinner with you."

About time, he thought. Her constant insults were growing thin. He turned to his housekeeper, who'd just entered the foyer.

"We will take our supper in the *sala*, Nelida. It is late. Bring the whole meal at once."

"*Sí, Patrón*," she replied.

"I will keep you apprised," he told Reyes. The man left with a nod, followed by the rest of the security team.

Marcos held out his arm. "This way."

Tamsin stared at his arm distrustfully. Her blue eyes, emphasized by the dark fringe of kohl and thick lashes, seemed as wide and deep as the sea. Taking his arm was obviously the last thing she wanted to do.

But, to his surprise, she gave him a smile before tucking her small hand in the crook of his arm. The glow in her expression was so unexpected it nearly took his breath away.

"Thank you." Her voice was a sultry purr, her eyes half-veiled by sweeping dark lashes, luring him on with the promise of some feminine mystery. Intrigued, he drew closer.

"Follow me, Miss Winter," he said, feeling off-kilter again.

She laughed, and it was as crystalline and pure as a melody. She touched him softly on the shoulder. "If I'm really going to be here for weeks, I think we can dispense with the formalities, don't you? Call me Tamsin. Marcos."

Watching her lush, full lips speak his name, he suddenly was hungry for more than dinner. In the space of a moment, the ice princess had become a fiery temptress and, in spite of his better judgment all he could think was that he wanted to throw himself into her flames.

But why the change in her behavior? Surely she wasn't that terrified of being locked in the tower?

Then it all became clear. She had changed her

strategy. Rather than insulting him, she thought she could charm him into letting her go.

It wouldn't work, of course. She took him for a halfwit if she thought he'd fall for such an obvious ploy. But, as she moved closer to him, her body swaying like music, he thought that after all her abuse of the past few hours it might be enjoyable for him to let her try.

He wouldn't be tempted by her, he told himself.

He was just curious to see how far she'd go.

Tamsin realized now that she'd been a fool to waste time with insults.

Unlike her pompous, rather oblivious half-brother, Marcos Ramirez wouldn't be baited so easily. He was smart, organized and ruthless. He'd gone all the way to Morocco to kidnap her. He'd obviously spent a great deal of time and money to set up his revenge against Aziz and her family. And she'd thought he'd let her go for being rude?

It was time for a new plan.

Marcos gave her a quick glance as they ascended the sweeping stone staircase towards the *sala*. His desire was plain in his eyes, though he quickly veiled his expression with a smile. He obviously believed her to be a shallow, promiscuous socialite. And, judging by the clothes he'd provided for her—a black Gucci halter dress with a plunging neckline and Christian Louboutin pumps—he'd been watching her for some time. The outfit was a duplicate of the one she'd famously worn to a party. It had caused the tabloids to proclaim her London's new 'it' girl—for that month, at least.

But now she wished with all her heart for a tracksuit

and trainers instead. The peep-toe heels in crêpe chiffon mesh, beautiful as they were, weren't exactly made to scale down stone walls or sneak past guards.

A sexy dress had other benefits, though. She glanced at him beneath her lashes. She could flirt with him. Lull him into complacency. Make him believe she might actually sleep with him.

Yes. She would deal with this arrogant Spaniard.

All she had to do was make sure Marcos continued to think she was everything the tabloids said—a shallow flirt who cared only for fashion and the admiration of men. She'd convince him that she was content to remain here in luxury while he prevented her marriage and ruined her family. Then, when his guard was lowered and he least expected it, she would escape to Morocco and stop him.

She smiled to herself, imagining the look on his face when his plans were destroyed by the woman he'd underestimated.

"Here we are," he said as they reached a wide dining hall. His hand lingered possessively on the small of her back.

"It's beautiful," she murmured, smiling up at him until her cheeks hurt.

It wasn't a lie. The architecture was medieval in appearance, though the plasterwork on the walls was covered with expensive modern art. She recognized a Picasso. The ceilings were high and the long darkwood table was decorated with a vase of exotic fresh flowers. The outside doors were open, overlooking a wide balcony and stone balustrade. She took a deep breath of night-blooming jasmine.

He escorted her to a seat near the end of the table facing the open windows. He was still wearing the same white shirt and fitted black trousers he'd had on the yacht, and she caught his scent on the breeze. He smelled of warm sun and Mediterranean sea and something else—something indefinable but totally male. Very different from Aziz, who wore enough cologne to make her gasp for air.

Marcos's scent, his body, his voice, all made her body hum with delicious tension. It was…confusing. How could she be attracted to him when she longed to crack him over the head with a heavy vase?

"Care for a drink?" he asked shortly.

She hesitated. "Yes. Thank you."

He went to the bar at the end of the dining room and her eyes followed his every step. Tall and broad-shouldered, he walked with lazy, sinuous movements, like a lion prowling the savannah. His crisp white shirt and finely cut trousers silhouetted the muscular shape of his body.

He turned back to face her. His strong jawline was dark with late-day shadow and his hair was black and full of curl. With his aquiline profile and full lips, his face was as perfectly chiseled and as cold in expression as a statue by Michelangelo.

Marcos Ramirez was a dark angel, she thought with a shiver. Beautiful, cruel and utterly without remorse.

"The brandy is from my own vineyards." He put her snifter on the table and sat next to her. She jumped when she felt his knee brush against her bare leg.

He quirked an eyebrow. "Did I startle you?"

She blushed in embarrassment, furious at herself for acting like the virgin she was. She tried to recover. "No. Your legs are just very…big."

"*Gracias.*"

So far, so good. She leaned forward to lightly brush her hand on his knee. "I admire strong legs on a man. Big hands. Big feet." She gave them a conspicuous glance. "So good for heavy lifting."

"I don't just have strength, but stamina," he observed, looking at her over his glass with an amused expression. "I can lift anything you want. All night."

Oh, my God.

Flirting with Marcos was very different from dancing with a pallid young earl or drinking with a bull-headed celebrity at a London club. Marcos was a full-grown man, and a dangerous one at that. She was his prisoner, in his castle. He could do anything he wanted with her.

Playing with him was playing with fire.

You can do this, she told herself. Make him think you want him. Act like the promiscuous woman he believes you to be. Lean forward and kiss him now.

But she couldn't do it. He was too powerful, too masculine, too in control of himself. It made her lose her nerve.

Grabbing her snifter, she lifted the brandy to her lips and drank deeply until the potency of the liquor caused her to choke and cough.

"Careful." He pounded on her back with his left hand. "Inexperienced with brandy?"

She *felt* inexperienced, and not just with brandy, either.

"I was thirsty," she responded lamely.

"Yes, I can see that." His gray eyes gleamed. "Are you hungry as well?"

"Very." She took another sip of brandy, more care-fully this time. "By the way, I owe you my thanks."

He regarded her with some suspicion. "For what?"

"For kidnapping me," she said, keeping her eyes wide with admiration. "For saving me from Aziz."

"Saving you? You were so desperate to marry him that you wanted to jump in the sea and swim back to Morocco."

"That was just because I was frightened. I didn't know what you meant to do to me. But I never wanted to marry Aziz—never. He would have stuck me away in the desert, a million miles away from shops, clubs, Harrods, everything." She shivered prettily. "What kind of life is that for a girl to lead?"

His lip curled. "*Qué lástima*, you are right. It would be a tragedy."

The only tragedy is how easily you're buying this, she thought. She leaned forward to put her hand over his. "I'm not your enemy, Marcos. I have no love for my brother or Aziz. Perhaps we can…help each other."

He glanced down at her hand. "What did you have in mind?"

His eyes had fallen to her mouth, and she licked her lips. Again, she had the feeling of being out of her league, out of her depth, and out of her mind. She couldn't manipulate a man like this. Could she?

She swallowed the last of the brandy with a gulp and held up the snifter, looking at him with her best smile. "Would you get me some more brandy?" She gave a little giggle. "My head is starting to spin in such a won-derful way."

Without a word, he took the glass and strode across

the old stone floor to the wet bar. She watched him with narrowed eyes, but the moment he turned back to face her she simpered at him, dimpling.

"Tell me your plans, and I'll tell you how I can help." She stretched her arms above her head with a dainty yawn, well aware that it would cause her breasts to rise against the low-cut halter dress. "I still don't understand why you think kidnapping me will hurt Aziz and my brother."

His eyes followed the swell of her breasts against the plunging black neckline. "It's enough that it will."

"But why do you want to hurt us?"

"Not you, *querida*. Them."

"Why do you want to hurt them?"

He shrugged. "They've got it coming."

Selfish bastard, she thought, irritated that he wouldn't explain further. *I won't let Nicole's life be ruined because of your stupid desire for revenge.*

Tamsin had already seen enough in her life, thank you, especially from her father's example. When he'd finally died of apoplexy, he'd been friendless and unmourned, and all Tamsin had felt was relief that he couldn't hurt them ever again.

"Here's your brandy." Marcos placed it on the table next to her.

"Thank you." She crossed her legs, trying to show them to their best advantage, then pretended to accidentally drop one of her high-heeled shoes to the floor. She leaned forward to pick it up, just to give him a nice view down her neckline.

When she sat up, he was looking at her like a hungry wolf waiting to devour a lamb.

Perhaps it had worked too well, she thought as he slowly walked around her. She could feel his hot stare move up and down her body and nearly jumped when his hands touched her bare shoulders. She hadn't expected her own senses to have such a strong reaction. Her voice trembled. "What are you doing?"

He smiled down at her, softly brushing her hair aside, causing shivers of awareness to spread from her scalp down her body. "You've had a difficult day, but we have the whole night ahead of us. To eat. To drink. To... enjoy."

Her heart gave a strange little thump as he massaged her shoulders. She felt his hands move lower on the bare skin of her upper back, rubbing the tense muscles around her shoulder blades. She closed her eyes, unable to resist leaning back.

"*Qué belleza*," he whispered. His fingers lightly traced the edge of her shoulder, the crook of her neck, the curl of her hair. "You are so beautiful."

"It's not me," she gasped. "It's just the dress."

"It's the woman in the dress." He bent forward to wrap his arms around her, pulling her against his chest. "Perhaps you are right," he said. "Perhaps we can help each other."

"Tell me your plans," she said, hardly able to believe that he was falling for her act, "and I will tell you how I can help you."

Running his hands down her arms, he gave her an enigmatic smile. "Perhaps. We shall see."

It was working! He thought he could trust her! But, just as triumph was coursing through her, the house-keeper and two waiters entered the *sala* with trays of dinner, interrupting them. To her chagrin, Marcos moved away to his own chair.

"I'm serving dinner all at once, as you wanted," the housekeeper said in Spanish, throwing a hard glare toward Tamsin. It bewildered her. Why would the housekeeper dislike her? "For your romantic night," the woman added sourly.

"Thank you, Nelida," Marcos replied in the same language, taking the tray from her. "I would be helpless without you."

The plump middle-aged woman looked mollified. "You'd starve, that's for sure. You'd live off coffee and *tapas*, or else forget to eat entirely. You always lose weight in Madrid."

"But I always come back so you can fatten me up. Good night, Nelida."

"I don't think your housekeeper likes me," Tamsin said after the woman and her assistants left.

"It's nothing personal," he said, buttering a thick slice of bread. "Nelida was my nanny when I was a child. She's old-fashioned and possessive. She doesn't approve of loose women."

Loose women! Tamsin thought indignantly. She looked down at her meal. "What's this?"

"The soup is *salmorejo*. Tomato soup, thickened with breadcrumbs, topped with chopped eggs and ham."

She hesitantly took a mouthful of soup. It was cold, but delicious. "It tastes like gazpacho."

"Yes."

"And this?"

"*Pato a la Sevillana*. Roast duck with onion, leeks

and carrots, cooked in sherry. And bread, of course. That's Nelida's specialty."

Tamsin took several bites and realized two things: first, that she was starving, and second, that if she were prisoner here for long she would soon be putting on weight too.

That was, if Nelida didn't decide to poison her for being *loose*.

She scowled.

"Do you like it?" Marcos's slate-gray eyes looked into hers, as if he were asking another question entirely. For a moment, his dark gaze drew her, pulling her into a trance.

She shook herself out of it. *Maybe I really am as stupid and shallow as he thinks*, she considered grimly. Why else would she be attracted to such a cold, cruel, heartless man?

She forced herself to turn her attention back to the food.

"It's delicious," she replied and quickly ate more. "Your housekeeper is a treasure."

Over the next hour, she fluttered her eyelashes and smiled, trying her hardest to get him to reveal why he'd kidnapped her, what his plans were, what her brother and Aziz had done to make him desire revenge. But, in spite of his hint earlier that he'd share his plans, he spoke little and revealed nothing. It was like talking to a brick wall. She continued to try, skimming her mind desperately for any topic that might make him open up—travel, business, even football. Finally, she gave up.

She'd never met such a brooding, unhelpful man in her life. Either that or she was losing her touch.

Fine, she thought resentfully. *If that's how you want to be, let's see how you like it.* She ate the rest of her meal in determined silence.

It seemed not to bother him a whit.

"You were hungry," Marcos observed when her plate was empty.

"Being kidnapped will do that to a person," she muttered, then gave a little laugh, as if it were a joke.

"Would you like more roast duck? Some dessert, perhaps?"

It was the most he'd spoken during their whole meal. But, unfortunately, any more roast duck and she'd burst out of her chic little dress. Another reason to wish she was wearing a track suit. "Thank you, but no. But there is something I do want."

He raised an eyebrow. "Your freedom, plus a quick flight to Morocco?"

She gave a nervous laugh, since that was exactly what she wanted. But she wasn't going to let him catch her so easily. Shaking her head, she folded her arms, resting them on the table with what she hoped was an earnest look. "I just want to know what my brother and Aziz did to you that made you so angry."

For a moment he looked as if he might tell her. Then he held out his hand. "Come out and see the view."

Reluctantly, she set down her napkin and let him draw her towards the open doors of the veranda. "You can see the valley all the way to the sea," he said. "See those lights? That's El Puerto de las Estrellas. The village used to be known for smugglers, pirates, thieves."

"Apparently it still is," she muttered.

His dark eyebrows lowered. "Perhaps so, now that

you are here. The Winters are liars and thieves, and your fiancé is worse."

She bit back a tart retort, knowing it wouldn't help her cause to argue. Besides…well, his accusation was true.

Sheldon had lied about many things. Particularly when he'd promised to watch out for Nicole. And, though she didn't know Aziz very well, she was reasonably sure he was keeping a mistress and intended to keep doing so after their marriage. Plus there was that other small matter of murdering his first wife.

As they stood on the wide stone balcony a cool breeze blew through the valley, making her shiver in her tiny cocktail dress. Without hesitation, he put his arm around her.

"I am glad you are here with me," he said softly.

Tamsin involuntarily leaned back into the warmth of his arms. Perhaps she had misjudged him, she thought suddenly. For all she knew, he had good reason to hate her family. Her brother and fiancé had certainly made enemies—even Tamsin despised them. Maybe trying to trick him and escape was a mistake. Maybe if she told Marcos the truth about why she was being forced to marry Aziz, he could truly help her…

"You are the pin in my grenade," he said, giving her a hard smile. "Without you, I could not destroy Aziz al-Maghrib and your brother so easily."

He was deliberately trying to bait her. She kept her expression bland, but inside she simmered. She wanted to kick him in the shins. Or maybe just kick herself for thinking well of him, if only for a moment.

What was it about him that kept luring her in? He

was as relentless as the sea. The darkness of his beautiful eyes held a dangerous riptide that tempted her to drown in the murky depths…

"Getting warmer?" he asked.

"Yes," she said, looking at him. The moon was covered with gray clouds. The only light came from candles in the dining room behind them. They cast a glow around the edges of Marcos's black hair, like a halo, leaving his face in shadow.

Dark angel, she thought again.

His gaze rested on her. "The cool air comes off the Atlantic at night."

From the height of the castle, she thought she could see a glimpse of moonlight on the distant ocean. Something square and hard rubbed against her hip and she glanced down beneath her lashes. She saw a glimpse of silver in his pocket.

His mobile phone!

If she had his phone, she could call Aziz. He could pick her up with his uncle's helicopter. Or she could call Bianca and Daisy, her two best friends from boarding school, who'd been her roommates over the summer. Bianca's wealthy family kept private jets in New York and London. Whether by Aziz's helicopter or Bianca's plane, she could be back in Morocco tonight.

She had to get Marcos's phone.

But how?

Kiss him, an inner voice whispered. If she could get him to put his arms around her, she could slip the phone out of his pocket. She would tuck it down her dress and make an excuse to leave. Then she could call Aziz and tell him where to find her. It was the perfect plan.

A shame she wasn't sure she could do it.

Kiss Marcos? She licked her lips nervously. She was accustomed to being the recipient of kisses, not the initiator. And Marcos seemed like the kind of man who would have a great deal of experience. Unlike her.

Feeling both awkward and bold, she forced herself to take his hand in her own. "What did my brother and Aziz do?"

To her relief, he didn't pull away. "Why do you keep asking me? Do you care?"

"I care because I hate them too. They're evil. Not just to me, but to someone I love."

Kiss me, she thought, looking up at him. *Kiss me*.

The way he looked down at her, pulling her close in the Spanish moonlight, almost made her forget why she was doing this. All she could think of was that they both hated the same men, and that she wanted Marcos to kiss her.

She slowly ran her hands down his chest. She could feel the muscles through his crisp linen shirt, feel the beat of his heart. "Tell me," she whispered. "Tell me what they did, what you intend to do in return."

He grabbed her hands, forced them to be still. His handsome face looked ferocious, almost savage.

Kiss me. She took the final step that pressed her body fully against his. She looked up. He was much taller than she was, but in this moment, as she looked up at him in the sultry jasmine-scented night, she realized she'd lost all fear.

"You aren't alone, Marcos." She pressed her cheek against his. His chin felt rough against her skin. Her lips brushed against his ear as she said softly, "Let me help you…"

She heard his sudden intake of breath. He pulled back, forcing her away from him.

"It won't work," he said harshly.

"What won't?" she asked, feeling dazed by her own sudden longing. All she could think about was him kissing her, feeling his lips on hers.

"Do you really think that you can just flirt and toss your hair and I'll be so dazzled I'll let you escape?"

Her cheeks burned red-hot. So he knew. He knew she was trying to lull him into letting her escape. "No, I—"

"I'm not that stupid. I won't let you go just for a few cheap kisses."

What was he trying to tell her? Shocked, she met his eyes. But she didn't have time to feel humiliated. She didn't have time to think. She was desperate—desperate enough to offer anything. She took a deep breath. "And what if I offered you more than just kisses?"

"Your body, you mean?" Apparently unaware of what it cost her to even suggest such a thing, he snorted in derision. "If I wanted you, I could seduce you. Easily."

"That's not true!" she gasped, hurt.

His dark eyes regarded her smugly. "We both know it is."

She ground her teeth. Perhaps it was true, that in her inexperience, she'd revealed that she wanted him, but she'd have died rather than admit it. "For your information, I've resisted much better men than you. Handsomer. Richer. Smarter."

"Have you?" he said evenly. He ran his hand

beneath her jaw line, forcing her to look up at him. "So if I were to kiss you now, you're saying that you would feel nothing."

"Not a thing," she said defiantly.

"Really." He wrapped his arms around her. Slowly, he lowered his mouth to hers, stopping when his lips were a millimeter from hers. "So this leaves you cold?"

She could feel his breath, smell the sweetness of brandy. Her lips felt swollen, tingling as if warming after frostbite, expanding towards his. "Completely."

"And this?"

He drew her to him in a hot, hard embrace. As he kissed her, her blood boiled, her body felt consumed by fire. Her bones went limp. Dimly, she could hear some inner voice screaming. There was something she was supposed to do while he kissed her. Something.

She felt his hands brush her bare back as he pressed her against the balustrade. His hips moved against her and she sighed beneath his mouth. She wanted something. What was it? To press her body against his? To let him lift her? To spread her legs and wrap them around his waist? To let him make love to her and finally learn the great mystery that most women her age already knew?

She felt dizzy in his arms. Trying to steady herself, she brushed her hand against his hip. She felt the small rectangle of the mobile phone in his pocket and her plans came rushing back.

His phone.

Later, she thought, dazed. Plenty of time for that later, after she'd had her fill of kisses…

But then she remembered Nicole's face, pinched and hungry as she'd seen it last month. She hated

Marcos for his cold arrogance, for kidnapping her, for keeping her in captivity.

So why was it so hard for her to stop kissing him?

Hardening her heart, she forced herself to slip the phone out of his pocket. Hiding it in the palm of her hand, she pulled away, looked him straight in the eye and lied.

"I felt nothing."

He blinked at her. His voice was hoarse as he replied, "You're lying."

"I'm a Winter," she said. "Just like you said. A liar and a thief." She took a step backwards. "Perhaps you should send me to the tower."

"Perhaps I should," he muttered, raking his hand through his hair.

She turned to go and, for a moment, she thought he was actually going to let her leave with her prize. Then he wrapped his hand over her closed fist, pinning her to the stone balustrade. "Wait."

"What?" Her heart was pounding. Any moment he'd discover that she was hiding his phone in her hand.

He bent his head to whisper in her ear and a pulse ran through her body as she felt his lips brush against the sensitive flesh of her earlobe. "I have to say, after all I've heard about your seductive skills, I'm disappointed. It was a clumsy attempt at best."

Oh! His insult left her vibrating with humiliation and rage. "You're the one who kissed *me*!"

He gave a derisive laugh.

"I just wanted to see how far you would go. Now I know. You've proved my point—you'll fall into my bed at the slightest provocation. So please don't try to bargain with your body again." His lip curled. "I can obviously get that for free."

She had to get out of here before he goaded her into saying something she'd regret. Still hiding the phone, she drew her hand away. Pressing her fist against the fabric of her skirt, she said furiously, "I'd rather be locked in the tower than spend another minute with you."

"Fine," he growled. "I'm sick of the sight of…" He stopped suddenly, his fingers tightening over her fist. "What's in your hand?"

"Nothing."

"Nothing!" He forced her fingers open to reveal the phone. Barking a laugh, he took it away from her. "Why, you conniving little tart." He looked at her in amazement. "You're even more clever than I thought."

Clever? She felt sick. She'd lost. It had almost killed her to laugh and flirt with the cold-hearted beast all night, but she'd done it. Now it was all for nothing.

But she couldn't let him see her anguish. Ignoring the hard lump in her throat, she raised her chin, glaring at him.

"Why else would I let you kiss me? Just being near you makes my skin crawl."

He gave her an amused smile, but his dark eyes glittered with anger and something more—bitterness? "And to think I almost believed your little show of compassion. 'I care, Marcos'," he mimicked. "'You aren't alone, Marcos'. You really are a Winter through and through—a thief and a liar. I almost believed that you actually hated Aziz."

"I wasn't lying about that!" she cried.

"Yes, you hate him so much you can't wait to throw

yourself in his bed. Fresh from mine, presumably. Tell me, does it ever get difficult to keep your lovers straight? Sleeping with multiple men each day must make it hard to keep count. Do you give out tickets, or do men just queue up outside your bedroom door?"

With a gasp, she drew back her hand and slapped him across the face.

CHAPTER THREE

MARCOS touched his stinging cheek. He'd deserved that, he supposed.

But, damn it, she'd played him like a guitar. And he'd fallen for it. Kissing her had been far too intoxicating. He should have expected it after their kiss on the yacht, but he'd told himself that was a one-off. He'd thought he was completely in control where Tamsin Winter was concerned.

He had been wrong.

"You owe me an apology," she said.

His eyebrows lowered. "I owe you nothing."

"I'm not the tart you think I am."

He gave an expressive snort.

She shook her head wearily. "All right, so I dated a lot of men in London. For the first time in my life, I wasn't under anyone's control, and I did exactly as I pleased. I didn't care what it did to my reputation. I stayed out all night, but I never fell in love with any of the men I dated. And I never—"

"Never what?"

She turned away. "Forget it."

Her face looked so sad, he almost moved closer. He felt drawn to comfort her. And, most of all, to kiss her again.

Dios mío, was there no end to her trickery? Did the woman have no shame?

Furious, he flung open his mobile phone.

"What are you doing?"

"Something I should have done hours ago. I'm calling your brother and Aziz to let them know I have you." Clenching his jaw, he tilted his head at her, pretending to consider. "Which one should I call first?"

"Neither!"

"Neither? You surprise me. Any normal woman would be begging me to call her family and friends, if only out of hope for a rescue."

She bit her lip. "I *do* want to be rescued. Only—"

"Yes?" He paused, his finger poised to dial.

"I'm afraid they won't rescue me," she blurted out.

"You think they won't care I've kidnapped you? They will. You're Aziz's betrothed, Sheldon's half-sister. They'll care about losing their business deal if nothing else."

Her eyes went wide. "You know about that?"

"Of course," he said impatiently, his accent thick. "Without the marriage, there will be no business deal. Winter International will be sold off for parts at a fraction of its worth, and both Sheldon and Aziz will be ruined."

"So that's why you kidnapped me," she said softly.

Irritated that he'd said so much, he clenched his jaw, glaring at her.

"But if Sheldon convinces the Sheikh to make the business deal without a marriage, your plan might not work," she mused, then took a deep breath. "Or if Aziz finds someone else to marry."

"Wouldn't that be a dream come true for you?" He lifted an eyebrow. "You can't honestly want to marry Aziz al-Maghrib. You're too smart not to know what life with him would be like."

"But I need them to need me. It's my only bargaining chip!"

"Bargaining chip for what?"

She looked at him with an expression he'd never seen before in her deep blue eyes: pleading. "Please, Marcos. Let me be the one to call Aziz."

"Why?"

She took two pacing steps. "He and I barely know each other, but I'm sure he has a mistress. I saw things in his room, heard a phone call he didn't want me to hear." She swallowed. "What if I don't show up for our wedding, and he just decides to marry her instead?"

Marcos frowned. "My investigators haven't found any evidence of a mistress. He's only been around you, Camilla and his sister."

Her jaw jutted stubbornly. "He has a mistress. I know I'm right."

"Even so, I doubt the Sheikh would find a low-class tart to be an acceptable bride for his nephew." He gave her a sardonic smile. "Present company excepted, of course."

Her lips pressed together and her hands clenched hard against the balustrade. "Insult me all you want, but let me call Aziz. Think of how much more devastating the call would be," she added in a wheedling tone. "I can sound frightened, tearful, whatever you want. I can say you've been maltreating me and beg him to save me."

"What are you really after?" he demanded. "What's your scheme this time—to give him clues about our location?"

"If that's what you're afraid of, I'll call him in front of you," she said. "I won't say anything you don't want me to say."

"I don't understand." He shook his head in disbelief. "Why are you so desperate to marry a man you claim to hate?"

She licked her lips. "I have my own reasons, which I don't care to share. Just as you do."

"Then I can't trust you." He started to dial Aziz's number on his phone—a number he'd involuntarily committed to memory long ago. "I have waited too long to—"

Abruptly, she snatched the phone out of his hands and threw it over the balcony. The two of them watched as it sailed through the night to land somewhere in the dark palm trees below.

She raised her face to look at him. Her eyes were wide. But, beneath her fear, she looked grimly determined.

He realized he'd made a grave mistake in ever believing that Tamsin Winter was a brainless coquette. He'd underestimated her. And while he'd complacently believed that he was the one in control, she'd been luring him towards his doom like some modern-day Circe.

But to what end? What was her plan?

No woman had ever intrigued him so much—or driven him so crazy.

"Why did you do that?" he asked slowly.

She gave a fake little laugh. "You don't want to call until after nine. Think of your mobile bill."

He grabbed her by the shoulders, causing her to cry out. "Why did you throw away my phone?"

"You're hurting me!"

His mood was dark, almost savage as he shook her. "Tell me."

"I just want to be the one to talk to him!" she cried. "He can't marry anyone else. I have to convince him I'm the only one he wants, or else my brother won't—"

"Won't what?"

"I love Aziz, all right? I love him, I miss him, I need to talk to him!"

"Liar! Love is the one thing you don't feel for Aziz." His lip curled. "You're playing me. And you've been doing it all night."

"I haven't—"

"What is your plan? Did you already find a way to contact your brother?" He gave her another hard shake. "Does Winter know that you are here? Answer me, damn you, or I swear I—"

"Please, no!" she shouted, cowering and protecting her face with her hands.

He stared at her. She was shaking. The blood had drained from her pale skin, leaving her white as snow beneath the black halter dress.

He realized that she believed he was going to hit her. It shocked him so much that he let her go. "*Madre de Dios*, Tamsin, I'm not going to hurt you."

"Just get it over with," she replied miserably.

He gently raised her chin. She still wouldn't meet his eyes but, as he turned her face towards the candlelight, he saw faded bruises along the side of her left cheekbone.

"Who hit you?" he asked in a low voice. "Aziz?"

"No," she whispered. "Not Aziz."

He knew at once.

"Your brother," he said grimly. "Winter did this to you."

She pressed her lips together and, when she finally looked up, her china-blue eyes were swimming with tears. "My father used to hit me all the time. At least Sheldon's only slapped me once." With an unsteady laugh she crossed her arms, pressing them against her body like armor. "I tried to run away with my sister. We didn't even make it out of Tangiers before he caught us. That's why he took us to Tarfaya. With the Sahara on one side and the sea on the other, he knew we wouldn't be able to escape before the wedding."

"Why did you try to run away?"

She didn't answer.

"Was it to avoid the wedding to Aziz?" His head was spinning. None of this made sense. "If the marriage is against your will, why are you so desperate to make it happen?"

"Why should I trust you?" she bit out. "You kidnapped me. You want to destroy my family. I'm not going to tell you anything!"

"The marriage is off. I won't allow your brother or Aziz to hurt you or anyone again."

She turned her face away. "It's not against my will. This past week, I...I changed my mind about Aziz. I don't mind marrying him. I...want to."

"You want to."

"Yes."

She was lying. He could see it in her posture, in the way she trembled in the warm Spanish night. "But Aziz has already been married once," he pressed, coming closer so he could see her face. "He beat that wife to death."

She licked her dry lips. "That was an accident. She was trampled by horses in the desert."

"Ah, yes, an accident." His voice was acidic. "It will be ruled an accident when it happens to you too." He heard her sudden intake of breath, but continued relentlessly, "Do you not care that your sister will grow up without you? Are you really so anxious to die?"

He saw her legs tremble and her knees start to buckle. Swiftly, Marcos pulled up a cushioned chair beneath her. She sank into it, looking fragile and bewildered.

Grabbing her brandy from the dining table, he pushed it into her hands. "Drink this."

"No."

"Drink it," he ordered.

She took a long drink, then gasped for air. "It feels like fire."

He brought a chair next to hers and, for a few moments, neither of them spoke. They looked out into the warm Andalusian night, over the moss-covered balustrade towards the dark, swaying palm trees and the distant lights of the village.

"Why are you suddenly pretending to be nice to me?" she asked quietly.

Her suspicious question almost made him laugh. In

his whole life, no one had ever accused him of being *nice* before. He shrugged. "You are my guest."

"But you want to destroy me."

"Your family, yes."

"That includes me."

He clenched his jaw, staring out into the darkness. It was true that he'd planned to take his revenge on Tamsin and her sister as well as Sheldon Winter. Though the sisters hadn't been directly involved in the ruin of Marcos's family—and in the younger girl's case, she hadn't even been born—he'd still hated them. He'd hated them for having everything that he'd lost. Security. Home. Money. Family.

Family most of all. He tightened his fists, remembering their last vacation. His brother Diego, always so serious and studious, had been running down the beach, trying to fly a kite. He hadn't been able to get the damn thing to fly, but he'd kept on trying. "Why can't you be like your little brother?" Mamá had sighed to Marcos, who'd been using his own kite as a target for rocks. Then she'd kissed him on the cheek with a warm glow in her brown eyes, as if to reassure him that she loved him even though he was a reckless scapegrace.

But by the next day her eyes had been red with weeping. And the day after that his whole family had died…

Marcos pushed it from his mind. He'd taken back nearly everything that had been stolen. Thanks to his venture capital firm, he had security and wealth. He had a flat in Madrid, an apartment in New York, an *estancia* in Argentina. He had a Gulfstream IV jet, an Aston

Martin, a Lamborghini, a Ducati. He had mistresses for the asking. He had everything a man could desire.

But, no matter how much money he spent, the emptiness never left him. It filled him like an ache. His only hope was that, by taking his revenge, the ghosts would leave him in peace.

He glanced at the girl sitting next to him. Her beautiful face was pale with misery. He could no longer see the smudge on her cheekbone, but that bruise had ruined everything. He'd set his sights on a proud, spoiled heiress who deserved a comeuppance—not a girl who'd been beaten, hurt, and nearly forced into a marriage against her will.

Unless, of course, this was just the latest in her string of lies. He tightened his jaw.

"I won't hurt you, Tamsin," he said coldly.

"How can you say that? You're hurting me now."

"If you mean by keeping you from marrying Aziz, then yes. I'm not going to allow that. Ever. So stop trying to convince me to let you go."

"I can't."

He shook his head in frustration. "Why? Because you hate him? Or because you love him? You've said both. Which was the lie?"

She looked at the flagstones on the balcony. "The only person I love is my little sister. I've never known anyone like her. She takes in stray animals and tries to nurse them back to health. When she has money, she gives it to homeless people on the street." She looked up at him, blinking hard. "She deserves a better family than us, but I'm all she's got."

Diego had loved animals too. Memories of his little

brother came flooding back so strongly that Marcos could barely breathe. He remembered how Diego had spent a whole year trying to convince his parents they should get a dog. He'd written up chore charts, read books on canine care and argued so eloquently that his parents had finally caved in. A week before Diego's tenth birthday, they'd shared a secret with Marcos: Diego would be receiving a dog for his present as soon as they returned to Spain.

But Diego had never lived to get his dog, since he'd died with his parents in that crash on the M25 outside London. Marcos later found out Diego had lived for an hour after the accident. He'd tormented himself ever since, wondering what that hour had been like for his baby brother. Wishing he'd been there to hold his hand. Wishing he'd had the chance to say goodbye.

Wishing he had been the one who'd died instead.

Marcos stood up abruptly.

"There," Tamsin said quietly. "I've told you the truth. Now tell me why you're so determined to get revenge against Aziz and my brother that you've dragged me here."

"It doesn't matter," he said coldly. "All that matters is that they're going to pay. Have you never wondered why Winter International is on the brink of bankruptcy? Your brother is the worst businessman I've ever seen but, for the last five years, I've helped. I've bought out his loans, subsidized his competitors, whispered criticisms of his leadership into the ears of his shareholders. And I made sure that all of Aziz's investments turned to dust and every gambling tip made him lose."

"You're the one who's caused Sheldon to go broke?" Tamsin suddenly looked at him with narrowed eyes.

"Tell me, do you have any idea how he's managed to maintain his luxurious lifestyle for the last few months?"

"I don't know and I don't care. Loans, I suppose. He's like Aziz—he only cares about status and money. Killing them would have been easier, but I wanted them to understand how it feels to lose the thing you love the most. I will take their fortunes and leave them broken. And for the rest of their lives they'll remember what they did to deserve it."

He stood on the edge of the balcony, his hands gripping the stone balustrade as he looked out blindly into the night. He nearly jumped when he heard her cold voice beside him.

"You're no better than they are."

Enraged, he whirled to face her. "What?"

"You're selfish and heartless. You hurt innocent people, crushing them down in your path."

"Like who?" he sneered. "Like you?"

"No." She said softly. Her beautiful eyes were wistful and sad. "But at least I'm old enough to take care of myself."

What the hell was that supposed to mean? Suddenly, Marcos had had enough of her mind games, enough of being caught off guard. Being in a prison cell sounded preferable to spending more time with this beautiful, infuriating, disturbing woman. "So you're still planning to escape?"

"Yes." Her eyes met his steadily. "You can't keep me here."

"Then let me help," he said brusquely. "I'll send Nelida to give you a tour. You can plan out your route."

He took several steps, then turned back with a brief humorless smile. "But fair warning, Tamsin. Don't ever kiss me like that again. If you do, I won't hold back. I won't be a gentleman. Offer me your sweet body one more time, and you're mine for the taking."

Tamsin paced alone on the balcony, fuming. She looked down from the edge of the balustrade. In the darkness, she couldn't even see the ground. She wondered whether there was any chance she could climb down the sheer drop of stucco and rock.

But at least Marcos had finally made his first mistake—having the housekeeper show her around the castle. Knowing the layout would help. With a little luck, she could still escape tonight.

The housekeeper gave her the tour. Tamsin had briefly studied medieval architecture at Smith, so she recognized the ancient Moorish floor plan, expanded and rebuilt repeatedly in the following centuries with modern amenities. And, in Marcos's case, his requirements apparently included guards, guards, and more guards, winding hallways that doubled back and a floor plan like a maze. Even the telephones required an access code to dial out of the castle.

He hadn't made a mistake asking Nelida to give her a tour, she realized. It was his way of showing her that she needn't bother trying to escape.

It only made her more determined to do so. When they were walking through the old portrait hall, Tamsin took her chance. "This seems like a very old place."

"It is," Nelida Gomez replied shortly.

"A place this old must have history," Tamsin said.

"Ghosts. Kidnappings." She added hopefully, "Old tunnels."

"There is one, but I'm not going to show it to you."

"Oh? Why not? I would love to…"

The housekeeper gave her a knowing look. "Because it begins in Señor Ramirez's room down the hall. And that's one place I have no intention of showing you. I suspect you'll find it all by yourself." Her accented English dripped with derision. "Here is your room." She opened the double doors and departed before Tamsin could make an indignant reply. "Ring for me if you need anything. I bid you goodnight."

Her bedroom was more like a five-star hotel than the dungeon cell she'd feared. An antique four-poster bed, decked in a luxurious blue canopy, faced a flat-screen television above the fireplace. Shelves of leather-bound books in different languages lined the wall.

Tamsin turned on a lamp and peeked in the closet. Hanging inside were new clothes her size in the exact same glamorous styles that she'd been photographed in by paparazzi. It was like looking into her own wardrobe back at her Knightsbridge flat. It was eerie.

How long had Marcos been spying on her?

Raindrops rattled against the windowpane, echoing across the room. She opened the window to breathe in fresh rain-scented air. In the distance, she thought she could hear the roar of the sea. She was also eye-level with the palm trees. A pity the trees were at least five stories high and positioned above rocks.

She closed her eyes. Marcos Ramirez seemed to have thought of everything. Even if she could get out

JENNIE LUCAS   59

of the castle, how would she contact Aziz? She didn't have a mobile phone, a passport, money.

She wondered what Nicole was doing right now. Were Sheldon and Camilla still in Tarfaya? Had they gone to the Sheikh's kasbah in the mountains? Or returned to England?

Did Nicole know that Tamsin had been kidnapped? Was she scared?

Tamsin still remembered how frightened she'd been when she'd held Nicole in the dark, cold mansion while her sister sobbed and clung to her. Knowing her sister had suffered alone had been like losing their mother all over again. But this time it hadn't been a terminal disease—or their cold, vindictive father—that caused that pain. Sheldon and Camilla had done it. Thoughtlessly. Cruelly. And all Tamsin had been able to think was: what if she hadn't gone to Yorkshire looking for her sister? What would have happened to her?

Her hands tightened. Sheldon, Camilla, Aziz, Marcos—she hated them all for their selfish arrogance, for putting her and Nicole in the middle of their war. She slowly opened her fists. Her palms were still covered with henna in the intricate design of a bride.

Angrily, she stuck her hands out in the rain and wiped them hard on her Gucci dress. The henna had been on her skin too long to smear, but the color faded slightly. She put her hands out again, leaning her head against the trim as she stared blindly through the open window. The water felt cold and fresh against her skin after a long day of dust and sea salt.

Then her eyes focused on something silver and shiny

in the darkness, hanging on the edge of the sharply sloping roof.

A second later, she kicked off her shoes and pushed the window as wide as it would go. As she climbed out on the slick tiles, rain pummeled her body, sticking her hair and dress to her skin. Somehow, she managed not to slide off the roof and fall to her death on the rocks below. Panting, she climbed back into her room.

For a moment, she cradled the prize in her hands, looking down at it with wonder, as if it were a lamp she could rub to make a genie appear and give her three wishes.

But she didn't need three wishes. She only needed one. Water dripped from her body on to the plush white rug beneath her bare feet as she used Marcos's mobile phone to dial a number in Morocco.

Marcos brushed dirt and wood chips from his hands. A fire crackled in the ancient stone fireplace of his bedroom, burning off the smell of rain. The temperature had dropped in the last hour. He glanced at the clock.

Nearly an hour had passed since he'd left her. Had she seen the castle? Was she already asleep?

An image of Tamsin in bed went through him with the force of a hurricane—her red-gold hair spread across the pillow, her pale, curvaceous body tangled in the soft white sheets. And she was just down the hall. Ripe for the taking. Hell, she'd thrown herself at him already.

He unbuttoned his shirt, yanking savagely on the buttons. He'd spent twenty years planning this revenge.

It would be stark lunacy to change everything now and sleep with Tamsin Winter. The girl was too smart and talented for her own good.

Bien, so she intrigued him. And he was attracted to her—hell, yes. He wanted her in his bed. Tonight. This minute.

Kissing her on the balcony, he'd felt the fire in her, barely contained. Her spirit was as bold and vivid as her hair. He wanted more of that. More of *her*.

And he wanted to be honest with her. She apparently had her own reasons to hate her brother. Why not make her his ally, when they shared the same enemy? As the saying went, *the enemy of my enemy is my friend*.

But that was the lust talking again, trying to give him an excuse to sleep with her. He wouldn't do it. He had to stay as far away from her as he could.

She'd told him too many lies already, and she was still holding back a secret.

He tossed his shirt in a crumpled heap on the floor. Sitting on his bed, he watched the heavy rain pound the windows. He pulled off his shoes and threw them across the floor. Getting closer to her would only cause complications, he told himself. He had to focus. Letting her call Aziz would create unnecessary risk.

Marcos would call both men himself, and inform them who'd kidnapped Tamsin and why. He'd dreamed of this moment for years. He'd waited long enough.

He reached for his telephone on his nightstand, then paused as he recalled Tamsin's tortured expression as she'd pleaded with him on the balcony. He hesitated. Furious at his own indecision, he rose from the bed and paced the room. The hardwood floor felt cool against his bare feet, the firelight warm against his chest.

He stopped two steps away from the phone, scowling down at it. Raking his hand through his hair in frustration, he abruptly turned on his heel and left his room. Without letting himself think, he went down the hall to Tamsin's room. With a single cursory knock, he pushed open her door.

His eyes went wide.

She was standing near the open window, soaking wet. Her dress and hair were plastered to her skin. She stared up at him in surprise. Dark kohl had dripped beneath her lashes, giving her the look of a bedraggled waif.

He crossed the room in four strides. She was shivering as he took her in his arms, and her skin was bone-cold.

He cursed under his breath. "What happened?"

For a moment, she didn't answer. Then her teeth chattered as she said, "I…I tried to escape. I thought I could climb out of my window and jump into the palm trees."

Something in her face didn't look right. She was lying, he thought. He knew full well that palm fronds were too flimsy for the weight of a cat. They were also at least ten feet from the roof, too far for anything but a suicide attempt.

But why would she lie about it? What could she possibly wish to conceal more than a failed escape attempt?

"Come with me," he ordered.

"No, I'm all right," she protested. "Really—"

Without a word, he lifted her in his arms and carried her to his room down the hall.

Placing her directly in front of his fireplace, he tried to warm her with his body, pressing his bare chest against the naked skin of her upper back. She felt cold, so cold. He set her down in the chair near the fire, wrapping her in a nearby blanket.

"I'm fine," she said, her teeth still chattering.

He pushed her into the soft cushions. Leaving her in the chair, he hit the intercom button.

"*Patrón*?" Nelida's voice replied immediately over the intercom.

"I need you to bring additional towels for my guest," he told her in Spanish. "As soon as possible."

"In her room?"

"No, mine."

Pause.

"Nelida?"

"Sí."

He saw a new wariness in Tamsin's face as he turned back to face her. He waited for her to challenge his order. "Is there a problem?"

"Um…no. I'm just wondering what you were talking about."

He was momentarily surprised until he remembered that she was still pretending not to speak Spanish. Probably because she knew it would help her escape if others spoke carelessly in her presence. A good strategy, he thought, but he was suddenly fed up with all the lies between them.

Standing in front of her chair so their knees nearly touched, he looked down at her grimly. "Tamsin, I know you speak Spanish," he said in that language.

"I don't," she protested in English.

He hid a smile.

"I saw your transcripts from Miss Porter's and Smith. You made excellent marks in Spanish. You studied it for eight years. So do me a favor, *por favor*, and drop the pretense."

Her face darkened. "How did you get my transcripts?"

"It doesn't matter."

"It's bad enough that you've been spying on me, but stealing my transcripts? Don't you have the slightest sense of decency?"

"No." He narrowed his eyes. "I've spent twenty years planning this. Do you think I care that you failed chemistry? I know everything about you. The clothes you prefer. The route your limo would take to your wedding. How vital your marriage was to the survival of your brother's company."

"Yes, well, you don't know everything," she muttered.

He instantly went on the alert. "What don't I know?"

She looked into the crackling fire.

He grabbed her shoulders. "What don't I know?"

"You're the one with all the answers," she retorted, yanking away from him. "You figure it out!"

He leaned forward. "Tell me," he demanded, his face inches from hers.

Even with her hair and make-up a mess, she looked beautiful, he thought. Like a princess from a story. Hair like fire, skin white as snow in the Pyrenees, eyes blue as the hot Andaluz sky. She was the kind of woman who could make a man lose all sense of reality. She could make a man lose a hundred years in a blink of an eye.

He'd had women in his life, but had never met one who so perfectly blended innocence and seduction. She made him soft and hard at once. It made him furious and lustful and full of yearning for something that he didn't understand. He shook his head, trying to clear his mind.

This wasn't just desire. It felt deeper. Almost elemental.

He pushed the thought away. What the hell was wrong with him? *It's just sex*, he told himself fiercely. He wanted her. Nothing more. If he had her in his bed, he would see that she was a woman like any other. Not magical in any way.

Maybe he had a good reason to seduce her after all…

He raised her chin, forcing her to look at him.

"I won't tell you a thing," she whispered. He watched the way her full lips moved, brushing against each other as she spoke.

"You will." He stroked her cheek. "You will tell me everything I want to know and beg to tell me more."

Slowly, deliberately, he lowered his mouth to hers. He kissed her until he heard a soft moan rise from deep in her throat. He stopped, looking down at her.

Her eyes were dazed.

"How do you do that?" She looked confused, almost frightened. "I've never been kissed like that before. Not by anyone. It scares me."

"Good." He was relieved to be in control again. For a moment, he'd felt strangely off-kilter. Poetic images of soul-stealing fairies and hundred-year days were from fantasies spun by his Irish-American mother, stories from the happy childhood he tried not to remember because it hurt too damn much.

But now they were on safer ground. Sex, lust, desire—those he understood. Those could be solved.

So why not just seduce her? Taking her to his bed, he could prove once and for all that she had no power over him. And find out the secret she was keeping.

Besides, damn it, he'd warned her not to kiss him like that again. She could have gone cold in his embrace. She could have pushed away. Instead, she'd kissed him back passionately, moaning in his arms. She wanted him as badly as he wanted her.

So why hold himself back like a saint? It wasn't as if the girl was a virgin, after all. Sleeping with her wouldn't have to change his plans against her fiancé and her brother. He would still take his revenge in spades.

In fact, seducing her might make it even more sharp and sweet. He smiled to himself, picturing Aziz's face when he realized that Marcos had taken full possession of his would-be bride…

A knock came at the door. Nelida entered with thick, luxurious white cotton towels, a box of matches and a bowl of rose petals. She went into the *en suite* bathroom and turned on the water. Two minutes later she left, closing the double doors behind her with an opinionated *harrumph*.

Marcos pulled the blanket off Tamsin's shoulders, dropping it to the floor. Taking her hand, he pulled her to her feet.

She had been looking avidly around the room, as if examining the architecture, but as he started to untie the top of her black halter dress, she put her hand on his, her eyes full of entreaty and fear.

"Let me help you, *querida*," he said softly.

"You want to help me take a bath?"

"I want you to be warm," he coaxed, massaging her bare shoulders. "You are cold, wet, miserable. You've had a difficult day, and that is partly my fault. Let me make it up to you."

"I'm not going to sleep with you, if that's what you think," she gasped, even while swaying like putty beneath his fingertips.

He paused. "Return to your room, then. I won't stop you."

She kept staring at the tiled walls and painted wood panels of his room. She must have been too nervous to meet his eyes, he thought. When she finally faced him, he understood why.

"No," she said. "I want to stay with you tonight."

Her honesty surprised him—and he gloried in her admission. Part of him wondered if she was hoping that spending the night with him would somehow help her escape. But, even knowing this, he found himself unable to resist. Taking her hands, he pulled her up from the chair. Her lips were moist, parted.

He'd warned her. Now, she would be completely his. He would learn all her secrets. Both of her body…and of her soul.

Brushing her wet hair to the side, he untied the halter and slowly unzipped the back of her dress. He could feel her shivering beneath his touch. Or were his own hands shaking? No, impossible. He wouldn't be that affected by a sexual affair. He always enjoyed them thoroughly, but forgot them just as quickly.

Her dress dropped to the floor, leaving only her white lace panties.

He sucked in his breath. She was exquisite, shaped like a houri, with full, high breasts, perfectly curved hips and a waist that could be spanned with his hands. It was all he could do not to take her in his arms, rip off the virginal white lace and press her against the wall. To kiss every inch of her skin and warm her with his breath, his lips, his body. To fill her with his heat.

One glance at her troubled blue eyes told him that wouldn't be the wisest move. She was still shivering, from cold or nerves or both.

He would take it slow.

First, he would calm her.

Then he would seduce her.

Taking it slow was the least he could do, he thought dryly, since he had no intention of giving her what she really wanted: her freedom. And, at this moment, looking at the pale curves of her body and beautiful, proud face, he couldn't imagine ever wanting to let her go.

CHAPTER FOUR

A MOMENT ago, Tamsin had been freezing. Now she felt as if she were on fire.

Marcos slowly stroked her body, his eyes dark with lust. His hands ran down her waist to the curve of her hips. Gently, he pulled her white panties down to the floor. Still kneeling, he looked up at her.

"*Qué belleza*," he breathed, and all she could think of was that she was naked in front of a man for the first time. She'd known that it would happen tonight, but she'd imagined Aziz taking her brutally in the dark, beneath a pile of blankets. This was totally different.

The fire caressed Marcos's body in rosy warmth. The light starkly illuminated the chiseled outline of his well-muscled torso above his pants. He was beautiful, she thought—her dark angel. Murmuring endearments in Spanish, he rose from the floor, slowly kissing up her body.

She closed her eyes, helpless to protest, helpless to move. A few hours ago, this man had been a stranger to her. An enemy of her family. Now he seemed intent on worshipping her, and she was allowing him to do it. What was wrong with her?

I don't have a choice, she told herself desperately. When she'd spoken with Aziz, he'd been so incensed at the blot on his honor that he'd wanted to bring his uncle's mercenaries to kill her kidnappers. Tamsin couldn't let that happen. It wasn't that she cared anything about Marcos, she assured herself, but it would be wrong to let his innocent servants take punishment with him. Even that rude housekeeper didn't deserve to be gunned down in cold blood.

So when Aziz had demanded to know the name of her kidnapper and her location, she'd said she didn't know. It wasn't *entirely* a lie, since the exact location of the castle was a mystery to her, but she'd arranged to meet him at El Puerto de las Estrellas at dawn.

All she had to do now was escape from the castle.

By some miracle, Marcos had brought her to his bedroom and, if the housekeeper had been right about the secret tunnel, it was a stroke of fate. She would distract him, find the tunnel and escape to the village.

She would even give Marcos her virginity if that was what it took. She had no choice. For Nicole's sake, she'd sacrifice anything.

But, as Tamsin felt Marcos's strong hands caress her body, she found herself wondering if it would even be a sacrifice…

She gasped as he touched her naked body. He took one breast in his hand, exposing her aching nipple, while his other hand traced like a whisper down her belly towards the tuft of hair between her legs.

Then his mouth came down on her breast, suckling her, and she lost all rational thought. His tongue swirled around her nipple, making her gasp and grip his shoulders. She threw her head back, closing her eyes as he devoured her with lips and tongue and teeth, bringing her to the edge between pleasure and pain. He moved to the other breast as his hand lightly teased her hips and thighs, grazing the edge of hair. A groan came from deep within her throat as she finally felt his hand reach between her legs. She nearly cried aloud with the strange ache of want. She ran her hands along his naked back, wanting him to touch her core—*willing* him to touch inside her…

Cursing under his breath, he moved his hand away.

"You make me forget," he said softly, looking up at her.

"Forget?" she gasped.

"Forget my plans for you."

"Plans?" Suddenly frightened, she drew back, trying to read his handsome, inscrutable face.

Standing up, he bent his head to kiss the sensitive crook of her neck, running his hands along her lower back, her hips, her backside. And she knew that, no matter how little she trusted him, she could no more tell him to stop than she could stop breathing.

He picked her up as if she weighed nothing at all. She leaned her head against his shoulder. *At last*, she thought. At last he would toss her on his bed, remove his pants, cover her with his naked body. She closed her eyes, aching for him, wanting nothing more than to surrender.

But he didn't take her to the bed. Instead, he carried her into an enormous bathroom of exquisite white tiles, lit by a dozen tall, tapered candles. He lowered her into the rose-covered bath and she sighed as the hot water enveloped her. She hadn't realized until that moment how grimy she felt, covered with rain and sea salt and the dust of two continents. Muscles she hadn't even realized were sore suddenly relaxed.

"Lean back," Marcos ordered. Obediently, she plunged her head back in the water and her cold, wet hair was submerged into warmth and pleasure. She sat up and rested her head against the bathtub's edge, feeling newly reborn. She was almost too relaxed to even care that he could see flashes of her naked breasts beneath the bobbing rose petals.

He sat on the floor behind her and poured a dollop of shampoo in his hands. He began to slowly massage it through her hair. She sighed again, more deeply. She closed her eyes, giving herself up to his ministrations.

"Rinse," he said, and she obeyed. Using a sea sponge and lavender soap, he began to wash her body, rubbing in a circular motion against her warm, rosy skin. He started at her shoulders then gently moved down her arms, her breasts, her belly, her legs. He pulled her feet out of the water, one at a time, massaging them deeply, then did the same with her hands.

Her whole body felt warm and dazed with contentment. She raised her hands in front of her eyes. The beautiful geometric patterns of henna that had marked her as Aziz al-Maghrib's bride were now so faded they'd almost disappeared entirely.

And it was as if shackles had fallen from her wrists.

If her plans went well, after tomorrow she'd be Aziz's bride. She'd be at his beck and call, enduring his fetid breath, his flabby body and cruel-fisted hands for the rest of her life.

But tonight was a different story. Tonight she was her own woman, free to feel joy and make her own choices.

And Marcos was her choice.

Whatever else she was forced to surrender to Aziz, she didn't want him to have her virginity as well. Before she was buried alive in the desert, she wanted one clear, pure memory of pleasure to sustain her for ever.

She wanted Marcos.

He made her feel things, want things, that she'd never known before. He went out of his way to make her feel warmth and comfort and pleasure.

Unlike Aziz, who would just expect her to pleasure him in bed and remain silent and cowed. He would beat her when he discovered she was no longer a virgin, but he would have beat her anyway on some flimsy pretext.

Making love to Marcos would be worth it. At that moment, she knew it would be worth any price.

"Ready?" Marcos asked, holding up a towel.

"Yes," she said, and it was true. *She was ready*. Ready for one night of freedom and joy before she destroyed her own life to keep her sister safe.

She stood up and rose-scented water sluiced down her body. Holding her hand, he helped her out of the tub. He brought her close in front of the fire, toweling off her body. Her heart beat erratically as he wrapped the enormous white towel around her. She could feel the warmth of his hands through the thick cotton towel.

He looked down at her. "Much better," he said softly.

"Much," she whispered, looking up at his sensual mouth.

He ran a finger lightly along her bottom lip.

"Tamsin, I make you no promises. To the contrary. We will have this one night together, a few weeks at most. After that, there can be no future relationship between us."

"Good." It would be too awful to see him again after her marriage to Aziz. Too awful to remember everything sensual and wonderful that she'd never feel again.

He raised a dark eyebrow. "Good?"

She couldn't explain, even if she'd wanted to. Hours felt short. She had such a limited, precious time to enjoy herself, to be wild, to be free. "Marcos, has anyone ever told you that you talk too much?"

He blinked at her. "You are the first woman to ever tell me that."

And you're the first man who will ever make love to me, she thought, but she didn't say the words for fear that they'd make him hesitate or hold back. He'd already tried enough to dissuade her. This was her night. Her decision.

Holding her arms out straight to her sides, she deliberately dropped her towel to the floor.

She heard his intake of breath. For a moment, he just looked at her and she could feel his eyes move over her body. Then he lifted her chin, lowering his mouth to hers in a warm, gentle kiss. Her breasts tingled, feeling heavy as they pressed against the hair of his muscled chest. She returned the kiss with fervor. His kiss became harder, more demanding.

The firelit room seemed to sparkle and swirl around her, like the night before her twenty-first birthday, when she and her friends Bianca and Daisy had drunk a bottle of champagne and spun around under the leaves falling from the bright October sky. Kissing Marcos was like that times ten. He tasted of champagne and passion and freedom. He made her dizzy, tipsy, drunk.

He lifted her in his arms and, still kissing her, gently set her on the bed. He stepped back and removed the last of his clothing. For a moment, he stood naked in the firelight, gazing down at her.

She stared back, blushing furiously but unable to look away. She'd never seen a naked man before. He was beautiful, rugged and hard and everything that she was not. And so big! What if she was clumsy? What if he laughed at her? Nervousness coursed through her.

But, when he came to her on the bed, his skin felt so warm against hers that her nervousness melted away. His muscled chest moved against her breasts. She felt him between her legs, pressing against her. He kissed her, swaying down her body, and she arched up towards him.

"Please," she whispered, not even sure what exactly she was begging him to do. She'd seen movies, of course, and read books, but experiencing it herself was overwhelming and strange. Nothing like she'd imagined...

"Wait," he said firmly. She felt his breath on her belly, then her thighs, and she nearly arched off the bed. He couldn't intend to—no, surely—

She felt his tongue between her legs. Delicately at first, then more greedily, he tasted her. He pushed her thighs apart and spread her wide. Her whole body felt tense, so tense, driving her forward as the first waves crashed around her and she cried out.

He lifted himself above her with his strong arms and, sheathing himself with a condom, he thrust inside her.

He was huge. The pain was immediate.

He stopped, staring down at her in shock. She looked up at him and, even while she was pummeled beneath conflicting waves of pleasure and pain, she knew she didn't want him to stop. She arched herself against him, raking her fingernails down his back.

"You're a virgin," he gasped.

She moved her body against his, teasing him with her breasts. "Not any more," she whispered shyly.

A tremor rippled through his hard body.

"I don't understand." His forehead creased. He looked younger, almost bewildered. "Everything I'd heard about you…"

"I tried to tell you." She couldn't let him stop now, didn't want him to pull away. She took one of his hands and slowly sucked the long length of his finger. "I was waiting. For you."

He sucked in his breath. As if unable to resist, he pushed into her again, slowly at first. She moaned as the pleasure began to overtake the pain. He thrust into her again, harder. He took her breasts in his hands, suckling her, biting her nipple. Tension coiled low in her belly. She threw her arms back, wrapping her legs around his hard-muscled buttocks as he thrust into her again and again, riding her hard and deep.

He gasped, his body slick with sweat, and cried out. Hearing him lose control sent her over the edge, and her scream joined with his as a second orgasm shook her body, even deeper and more shattering than the first.

Afterwards, she held him in a daze. His arms were tight around her, his skin warm against hers. She could hear the crackling of the fire.

At last she understood why he'd warned her there could be no relationship between them. Because, at this moment, she felt so warm and dazed and protected and loved, all she wanted to do was to stay in his arms for ever.

But she had an appointment at dawn. Not with a firing squad, but close.

"I was wrong about you," he said softly, holding her close.

"Yes."

He took a deep breath. "I accused you of horrible things, and the whole time you were a virgin."

"It's all right."

"No, it's not. I kidnapped you, blamed you for crimes that were not your own, then insulted you." Still stretched out on the bed, he stared up at the ceiling. "I was wrong."

He looked so angry with himself that she wanted to soften the blow. "I was careless with my reputation," she pointed out.

"But I should have known. For ten years I've had reports on you, the kind of girl you were growing up to be. I shouldn't have been so quick to believe the worst." He looked at her and added in a voice so quiet that she had to read his lips in the firelight, "I owe you an apology."

His words were halting, hesitant, as if spoken in a language he barely remembered from his childhood.

She stared at him in shock, wondering if it was the first time he'd ever apologized to anyone.

"What was it you said?" he muttered. "That I crush innocent people to get what I want?" He looked down at her with a sudden ferocity in his eyes. "Is that why you gave me your virginity? Did I force you some-how?"

"No!" No matter how much she wanted to escape, no matter how much she needed to find the secret tunnel, she couldn't let either of them believe that. "I wanted you. You're the first man I ever really wanted. And I don't regret it. I don't regret it for a second."

At her words, the hard line between his brows slowly melted away.

"Thank you," he said quietly. He kissed her on the temple. It was a gentle kiss, pure, and somehow it affected her more than all the fiery, passionate embraces that had gone before. "I will make it up to you, Tamsin, all the wrongs I've done you. For the rest of your time here, I will treat you like a princess. Like a goddess."

He kissed her again, caressing her cheek and stroking her hair. For long moments, he held her in the flickering firelight, her head cuddled against his shoulder. Without moving her head, she glanced up at him.

His eyes were closed, but there was a small smile still on his lips. He didn't look like the grim brigand of the desert. He looked boyish, relaxed.

He looked like a man she could love.

Oh, no, she thought. Love Marcos? She couldn't let that happen. It would already be difficult enough to leave him after what she'd just experienced in his arms. Surely she wasn't stupid enough to allow herself to fall in love with him? No!

No woman ever forgets her first lover, she told herself. *That's all.*

She had to find the secret tunnel and leave. Tonight. She had no choice. She'd put it off long enough.

"You…you said this was once an old Moorish castle?"

"Yes." His voice was contented, sleepy.

"What's the oldest part of the room?"

"Hard to say. It's been expanded and rebuilt for hundreds of years. That wall is probably the oldest." Blinking, he nodded towards the side of the room near the old fireplace, which had heavily ornamented wood panels. "Why, *querida*?"

For the first time he spoke the endearment sincerely, without a single trace of irony. The tenderness in his voice made her heart ache.

"I've always been interested in architecture," she said over the lump in her throat. "You know that. You've seen my transcripts." There was one design in particular that drew her attention. A large oval, bedecked with geometric designs and tiny birds. That could be a door, she thought.

She started to rise from the bed.

His hand on her arm tightened. "Where are you going?"

"To look."

"Stay here," he said, pulling her close. "Stay and sleep with me."

"I need a nightgown," she improvised.

He pressed his naked body against her own. "I like what you're wearing now."

So did she, but that didn't matter. Nothing mattered now but finding the secret tunnel and saving her sister. "But what if the servants were to see me like this?"

"It would be their luckiest day on earth and they would bless the heaven that gave them such a vision."

"Nelida already thinks I'm a tramp."

"A mistaken opinion that will change, I assure you. She will come to respect you as I do."

"Not if she sees me loitering naked in the hallway, she won't. She'd have me strung up by the neck as a warning to other would-be tarts."

"*Bien*," he said with a mock sigh. "I see that I am out-gunned. I'll get your nightgown, milady."

The instant Marcos left the room, she leapt from the bed. She had only seconds before he would return. She ran her fingers along the edge of the panel in the wall. It was a door! Hidden to one side, behind a lamp, she found an old lock. But where was the key?

She looked wildly around the room. His desk! She ran to the desk and threw open the drawers. Any moment now, he'd return. If he caught her digging through his belongings, the jig would be up, as Daisy would say.

She heard a door slam down the hall. Her fingers felt a ring of keys, including one oddly shaped skeleton key. She heard his footsteps returning. Leaving the keys in his desk, she threw herself back into bed the very moment the door opened. She closed her eyes, pretending to be half-asleep as he climbed back into bed.

He lightly stroked her hair. When she looked up at him, he tucked the nightgown against her breasts.

"I haven't been surprised by anyone in a long, long time," he said softly. "Why?"

"Why what?"

"Why did you give me your virginity after the way I treated you?"

"I told you. You were irresistible." She continued to smile, but inside she felt weary. Just the thought of leaving him was already killing her.

He laughed, and the sound was so open and trusting that it made her throat hurt. "Irresistible, eh?"

"Sí." She gave him her best approximation of an impish smile.

"Aha. So you do speak Spanish." He returned her grin. "I wish you'd trust me with the rest of your secrets, Tamsin. I know you think you can't, but you can. Your brother and Aziz are the ones I want to hurt. Not you. Whatever hold they have over you, let me help. Let me protect you."

It was so tempting to tell him everything. How wonderful it would be to simply trust Marcos to protect them, to save her young sister and release them both from Sheldon and Aziz's power. Tamsin would be free to live the rest of her life however she wanted. Free to spend the rest of her nights in Marcos's bed.

There can be no future relationship between us.

I intend to destroy your fiancé and your family, and you're going to help me do it.

"Marcos, I'm too tired to talk," she said, pulling the nightgown over her head. "It's been such an eventful day. I just want to go to sleep."

With a sigh, he caressed her hair with his hand. "*Bien, querida.* Tomorrow."

Lying next to her in bed, he held her close. She closed her eyes, pretending to sleep. After a long while, she heard his breathing change. Opening her eyes, she watched him sleep in the dying firelight.

Darkly handsome, with a chiseled profile and a deep

shadow along his jawline, he looked different to her now. He slumbered like a boy, with a soft smile on his lips.

Her heart in her throat, she crept out of his arms and went to his desk. She took the skeleton key out of the drawer and went to the lock on the wall. The key fit perfectly, unlocking the hidden door. It swung open without a squeak.

Fate, she thought, feeling sick. She'd been selfishly hoping the key wouldn't work. Or that it would make so much noise in the lock that Marcos would wake up, sweep her back into his arms, and she'd have no choice but to stay.

But Aziz was waiting for her. And so was Nicole. Were Sheldon and Camilla feeding her? Keeping her warm? Telling her every day how much they loved her?

She doubted it.

Tamsin had had one selfish, glorious night. It would have to be enough. From now on, her sister would come first.

With one last regretful glance at Marcos, she took a deep breath and crept barefoot into the cold, musty darkness of the tunnel.

Marcos woke up alone in bed.

His bedroom was dark. It was still so early that no birds were singing.

He could smell her scent on his pillows, his sheets. He stretched his arms, yawning. He felt so good. Even though it was technically still night, he'd already had the best sleep he'd had in ages. Lazily, he stretched his arm across Tamsin's pillow. Where was she? he wondered. In the bathroom? Downstairs, hunting for an early breakfast?

He wished she would hurry back. He was hungry too, and not for food. Her lingering scent was like an aphrodisiac. Dawn hadn't broken over the horizon and he felt as excited as a boy on Christmas morning.

Tamsin had given him her virginity.

He still couldn't believe it. He hadn't thought there was such purity and innocence left in the world. It was a gift, one he'd neither expected or deserved. Even the prospect of taunting Aziz and Sheldon paled next to the delicious idea of staying in bed with Tamsin all day.

Pulling her pillow against his chest, he waited for her to return.

Twenty minutes later, his smile had faded to a glower.

Climbing out of bed, he looked in his expansive bathroom, then crossed the hall to call her name. His voice echoed against the walls of her empty, darkened bedroom.

The first cold trickle of fear cascaded down his neck.

She could be trying—unsuccessfully—to flirt with his guards, he told himself. She could even be roaming the halls, looking for a way out. Any of that was fine. After all, she'd just slept with him. She hadn't promised she'd stay.

But she couldn't still be trying to escape. Could she? No. Not Tamsin. She wouldn't give one man her virginity and then rush to marry a different man the next morning.

Would she?

Besides—he shook the thought out of his head—

even if last night hadn't meant anything to her and she still wanted to escape, there was no possible way she could.

Pulling on a T-shirt and jeans, he did a quick search of the main castle hallways. He spoke to his night guards, but they hadn't seen her.

By now his hands clenched with escalating rage and fury. He woke up Reyes and everyone else in the house. If he had to be awake and searching for her then, damn it, so did they. He ordered them to begin a thorough, methodical search that he already knew would be useless.

She was gone.

She'd tricked him.

All the time he'd thought he was seducing her, she'd really been seducing him. She'd coldly traded him her virginity like a commodity and while he'd slumbered like a trusting, contented fool, believing he'd found an angel, she'd disappeared from the castle like a ghost.

He stormed back to her bedroom. Cursing under his breath, he started digging through the wardrobe, looking for an explanation. Looking for a clue she might have left behind. All her clothes were still hanging in her closet. Her bed was perfectly made. There was nothing anywhere to hint how she…

Then he saw the glint of his mobile phone, hidden beneath the table by her window.

Snatching it up, he found the last number she'd dialed and swore loudly.

When he'd found her here last night, she'd been soaking wet, surprised and panicked by his sudden intrusion. He'd known something was wrong, had known her explanation about a failed escape attempt was a lie, but he'd ignored it. He'd thought he could seduce her into telling him the truth.

Now the truth was smacking him across the face. She had found his phone on the roof and climbed out into the wind and rain to get it.

Marcos had lost her, had lost everything, for one night of pleasure. He'd destroyed everything because he'd been so damned eager to get her into bed. And Tamsin, in sacrificing her virginity, had proved to be a more coldly ruthless competitor than he'd ever imagined possible.

He hadn't been wrong about her when he'd believed her to be a heartless coquette and calculating harlot. That was exactly what she was. She'd used her virginity against him, and now he felt like the one who'd lost his last vestige of innocence and hope. He'd fallen for her scam like some green eighteen-year-old boy.

But how had she escaped?

Taking the phone, he stomped back to his bedroom as his mind went furiously from one possibility to another. He trusted his men with his life. None of them would have let her go. None would have fallen asleep on duty. There was no way she could have climbed down the sheer rock of the castle. Was she truly a magical creature who could just disappear?

His eyes fell upon the wood panels of his bedroom wall. The geometric designs were barely visible in the gray shadows of the morning, but for some reason it drew his attention.

The old tunnel?

He went straight to his desk, but couldn't find the

key. With growing apprehension, he tested the door. It fell open, unlocked. Just inside the tunnel, he saw the key in the scattered dust of the floor—exactly where she'd left it.

The curse that exploded from his mouth was loud enough to be heard across the castle. How had she known? How could she possibly have known? He stormed down the hall, yanking on his shoes as he walked.

Nelida must have told her. He'd known the old woman disapproved of him taking lovers—she adamantly believed it was time he settled down and started a family—but he'd never thought she'd work against him this way.

"You're fired," he growled when he passed her in the hall.

"It's better this way, *Marcosito*," she replied serenely, not believing his threat for a second. "You don't need a trampy woman in your life. Get married. Find a good wife."

Grinding his teeth, he found Reyes in the foyer.

"*Señor*?" Reyes answered promptly.

"Stop looking inside the castle. She's gone," he snapped. "Organize the men to search the countryside."

Before the man could reply, Marcos strode away. His only hope was to find Tamsin before Aziz did. Dawn was just a blood-red smudge on the horizon as he roared down the hill in his red Ferrari. On a hunch, he turned left on the slender winding road to the nearest village, El Puerto de las Estrellas.

Please, he thought. *Please*.

He was too tense to be angry. Too tightly wound to

be furious. He just had to find her. He *would* find her. He hadn't planned this for twenty years to fail now. He hadn't made love to her last night, hadn't slept in her arms, just to see her become Aziz's wife.

He drove around the corner and, like a miracle, he saw Tamsin running out of the shadowy trees on the western edge of his vineyard. She was still wearing the white nightgown from last night and her red hair was flying free behind her. She was headed straight towards the village on the seaside cliff.

Gunning his Ferrari, he roared up on the road in front of her, blocking her path. He stopped his car in the middle of the road and jumped out.

With a stifled scream, she turned and ran back through the long, even rows of his vineyard. Grimly, he pursued her. With every step, the memory of how she'd tricked him, how she'd betrayed him, pulsed through his blood. Everything she'd said, everything she'd done, was a lie. He'd known he couldn't trust her. And yet, while he'd been humbly asking her forgiveness and promising to treat her like a princess, she'd been slyly angling for the secret door.

"Stop!" he shouted.

But she kept running, zigging and zagging across the rows, crawling under the full branches of the heavy Palomino grapes. He saw a trace of red left in her footprints across the sparkling dew of the white, chalky *albariza* soil. Her feet were bleeding, he realized. She was barefoot.

This enraged him even more. How had a mere girl, armed with nothing more than beauty and courage, managed to escape his power, his guards, his technology?

"¡Pare!" he roared again, but she just gave him a glance like a terrified deer and ran for the cool, dark orange grove on the edge of the vines.

She was barefoot, but she was fast. Clenching his fists, he cursed aloud and quickened his pace. He broke into a run before he finally caught up with her in a thicket of tall, overgrown trees. As he grabbed her shoulder, he was so furious he could barely control his rage.

"What do I have to do?" he demanded. "Lock you up and throw away the key?"

"Try it! I'll still escape!" She whirled around, panting. Her full breasts, barely covered by the thin white cotton, rose and fell with every quick breath. Her cheeks were rosy and her blue eyes glittered with fury. "You can't hold me!"

Even in the darkness and chill of early dawn, he could see her taut nipples through the thin fabric. "Why are you so determined to marry Aziz?"

"Perhaps I miss his touch after spending so much time with a man like you—ah!"

He'd pushed her against an orange tree, slamming his body against hers. Several oranges rained down from the branches on to the earth. "A man like me? What kind of man am I?"

"You're as bad as the others," she gasped, and he could feel the softness of her curves against him, driving him wild with every breath. "You don't care if you hurt people, so long as you get what you want. If you had any kind of heart, you'd let me go!"

"Heart?" he snapped. "You traded me your virginity on a silver platter. You seduced me in order to escape, making me think I could trust you, you cold-hearted, mercenary little liar—"

"I had no choice!" she cried, even as he saw her eyes lower to his mouth. "You forced me—"

Forced her? That was the last straw. "Call it what you like," he ground out. "I'm a selfish bastard who seduced you against your will. I took your virginity. I took my pleasure. And I intend to do it as often as I please."

He lowered his lips to hers in a punishing embrace.

He felt her gasp beneath his touch. Helplessly, she pushed against him, but he was too strong for her. She tried to keep her mouth closed, but he forced her lips open, pushing his tongue brutally between her teeth.

Suddenly, she relaxed in his arms. Small hands that had been battering against his chest clenched his shoulders as a low moan rose from deep within her. The kiss matured into a long, passionate caress as he ran his hands along her waist, her hips, and finally her backside. He was lifting her against the tree and had already pulled her nightgown up to her thighs when he remembered that they were near the road, hidden only by the small copse of orange trees. Aziz and his thugs were likely nearby, looking for them.

What was it about this girl that made him lose his mind?

"We'll continue this discussion later," he growled. She blinked up at him, her limpid blue eyes looking dazed as he lifted her up in his arms and tossed her over his shoulder like a sack of potatoes.

"Wait—no!" she cried, and started to struggle and kick.

Ruthlessly, he carried her through the trees towards the road.

"Please," she screamed, and her voice ended with a sob. "You have to let me go."

"Why should I?" he demanded.

"Let me go or my sister could die!"

That stopped him in his tracks. He could already see his car through the trees, but he immediately put her down. "Tell me," he ordered.

She shook her head miserably.

"Another trick. I knew it," he said, and started to reach for her again.

"It's not a trick!" To his alarm, her eyes filled up with tears. "You were right when you asked if I was marrying Aziz against my will. My brother is forcing me. I have no choice!"

"What hold does he have over you?"

"Nicole—she's only ten. I thought that she was being cared for by our nanny, but last month I found out that Sheldon used his power as trustee to ransack my trust fund. Now he's doing the same with hers. I found Nicole half-starved and alone on his Yorkshire estate, while he and Camilla were using her money to ski in Zermatt."

Marcos shook his head, clenching his jaw, wondering if he should believe a word out of her beautiful, lying mouth. "And your brother convinced you that if you clinched his business deal by marrying Aziz, he would take better care of your sister?"

"As if I would believe that." She wiped tears from her eyes savagely. "My brother promised that, if I married Aziz, he would give me custody and guardianship of Nicole. She couldn't live with me, of course, but I could use her trust fund—what's left of it—to hire back the nanny and make sure Nicole was loved and safe."

He stared at her with shock. "But you would be trapped for the rest of your life! Aziz would never let you go, Tamsin. As his wife, you would bear his name, bear his children. You would be his possession until the day you die. He'd value you less than his horses and treat you accordingly." He furrowed his brow. "You would really sacrifice yourself for your sister?"

She looked up at him miserably. "My sister is ten years old. Ten, Marcos. She's a better person than I ever was. She deserves to be protected and if I don't do it, who will?"

It left him speechless.

Ten years old. So young. His own brother had been nearly that age when he'd died, and there had been no one to protect him. Certainly not Marcos. He hadn't helped his little brother, he'd only caused his death—

Marcos pushed the thought away. He looked at Tamsin grimly. "Marrying Aziz is a death sentence."

"But what else can I do?" Tamsin said, clutching her hands. "If you have a better idea, I'd love to hear it."

He clenched his jaw. "Go to Social Services in Britain and fight for custody."

"You think they would give custody to me, the party girl of the West End? They'd just toss her into foster care. I can't let that happen. For most of my life I was in America and barely saw her. I called, sent gifts on her birthday, visited on holidays. I trusted that my stupid, selfish brother would take care of her." She folded her arms, raising her chin. "So it's my fault that she was half-starved and abandoned. *My fault*. I should have been looking out for her."

"Right," he said acidly. "But after Aziz kills you in another little *accident*, your sister will be as alone as ever. She won't even have you to protect her. What will happen to her after you're dead?"

She stared at him, tears welling up in her eyes. "I...I don't know."

Marcos heard a loud slam. He looked at the road and saw a beat-up van. Four hard-eyed guards were pouring out of the back of it with guns. Aziz al-Maghrib, dressed in the traditional white robes of a sheikh, descended from the passenger side door as if he were going to a party.

He *was* going to a party, of sorts. Marcos's funeral.

Marco grabbed Tamsin's arm and forced her to kneel low against the ground, where the younger orange trees, as well as scrub bush like lavender and rock rose, offered more cover.

For all the good it did to hide with his Ferrari sitting parked on the road, shining a brilliant red in the first light of dawn.

¡Maldito sea! He cursed himself for a fool. He'd left himself only two options.

He could fight.

Or he could run.

He watched two guards begin a methodical search of the vineyard, while the other two came towards the grove of trees. His Arabic was rudimentary, but he understood enough of what Aziz was shouting at his men to know that his chances of escape were grim. Either Tamsin had told him who'd kidnapped her, or Aziz had guessed. But at any rate, they'd recognized his Ferrari.

He knew he could disarm and disable one man, and perhaps two, but he wouldn't stand a chance against five armed men at once. Chances of Marcos getting a swift bullet to the brain or heart were high. And, though Aziz hated to get his hands dirty, preferring others to do it for him, Marcos had to grudgingly admit that the man could fight. He was cunning and vicious and, while at the University of Paris, he'd learned *Savate*, the French martial art combining street-fighting and kickboxing.

Even Marcos knew he couldn't fight Aziz and four other trained fighters at once and win.

And as for running away?

Marcos knew this forest, the vineyards, every inch of his land. If he let Tamsin go, it would distract Aziz's men long enough for him to escape.

But he looked down at Tamsin in his arms. She was pale. The only color in her face was her bright pink lips. She was biting down on them hard, as if to keep from screaming, while her eyes followed Aziz's every movement.

Give her up to Aziz? Fail after twenty years? Let the man who'd destroyed his family continue to live in peace and prosperity—with Tamsin as his wife? Give her to Aziz, to be in his bed every night, to use her how he pleased?

No. Marcos clenched his jaw. He'd rather die than let that happen.

Holding tight on to her, Marcos whispered in her ear. "This is your chance. One scream from you and they'll find us. They'll take you back to Morocco. You'll be Aziz's bride before the day is out."

She visibly swallowed. "And you?" she mouthed.

Clenching his jaw, he glanced towards the nearest guard. He was drawing closer, pushing through the trees. "They brought those guns for a reason." He looked back at her. "One scream, and this will all be over."

CHAPTER FIVE

MARCOS looked so grim, Tamsin thought with a cold shiver. Almost as if part of him hoped that she really would scream.

Staring at Aziz's men through the trees, she opened her mouth, trying to make herself do it. Aziz would take her and, Marcos was right, she'd be his bride by the end of the day. She could ensure her sister's safety.

But for how long?

After Aziz kills you in another little accident, your sister will be as alone as ever. She won't even have you to protect her. What will happen to her after you're dead?

She would just have to stay alive, she told herself desperately. She would obey Aziz's every whim. She would please him in every way…

She glanced at Marcos. His eyes were dark and unreadable. She made a small noise in the back of her throat, and he didn't even flinch. She could scream, she realized. He had no intention of stopping her.

But if she screamed, what would happen to him?

"Tamsin," she heard Aziz sing softly from the road. His crooning voice made chills run down her spine. "I know you're here, *ma petite*. Does he have you? Do not fear. We'll soon find you. Both of you."

Shards of sunlight were starting to penetrate the edges of the orange grove. The two nearest guards came closer. Fallen branches cracked beneath their boots like gunshot.

Even if she remained silent, they wouldn't be able to hide for long.

Marcos's eyes suddenly narrowed. Very quietly, he pulled his mobile phone from his pocket. She watched him, breathless with sudden hope.

"Reyes?" she mouthed, and he nodded. As he punched the keys, the tiny screen had a fluorescent glow. Tamsin cradled her hands around it, trying to hide the small light. Haltingly, Marcos started to text a message, his large fingers clumsy against the keys.

She put her hand on his arm, looking at him beseechingly. With a breath, he nodded and handed her the phone.

With practiced swiftness, Tamsin swiftly texted a message. She handed him the phone so he could see what she'd written. He nodded, then hit 'send'. He closed the phone with a soft click.

Meanwhile, Aziz's bodyguards were coming closer. She heard one of them say something in Arabic, saw him pointing at the ground. Aziz gave a loud, guttural order and the two men in the vineyard gave up searching the rows and came to join them in the orange grove. What had the man seen on the ground? She bit her lip. Had they dropped something when Marcos had chased her?

Then she glanced at her feet, tucked underneath the muddy, bedraggled hem of her nightgown. Her hand rose to her mouth to cover her sudden intake of breath.

Her right foot had a deep cut on the sole. She hadn't felt it—her feet were half-numb. But she'd been tracking blood with every step.

The blood would lead Aziz's men right to them. The sun was rising and, with every minute of the new day, the grove was growing brighter. Soon there would be enough light for Aziz to see the path.

She grabbed Marcos's hand, pressing it to her heart. At this moment, all she could think about was that she didn't want Aziz to find her. She didn't want to leave Marcos's side. Most of all, she didn't want him to die.

She glanced back at her foot and he followed her gaze. His expression was grim. Clenching his fists, he slowly stood up, and she could read the resolve in his eyes.

He intended to fight for her.

But, as powerful as he was, he was only one man against five. She couldn't let him sacrifice himself for her. Aziz would destroy him.

She rose to her feet, squaring her shoulders. She took one step forward, steeling herself to run towards Aziz.

He grabbed her wrist.

"No," he whispered.

She shook her head, wanting to cry, but there were no tears left. "It's the only way I can save you."

"No," he repeated more loudly. This time there was an edge of steel to his voice.

One of Aziz's men looked up, tilting his head as if he'd heard something. She swallowed, feeling torn apart. Marcos wasn't going to let her give herself up to Aziz, but what did he expect her to do? Watch calmly while they gunned him down in front of her?

She heard the sound of an engine down the road. It was false hope, she told herself. Probably just a plane flying overhead. But, like a miracle, the sound grew louder, and one of Aziz's men suddenly shouted an alarm. She heard Aziz curse loudly in French, then watched as he turned in a furious, haughty swoosh of robes. At his orders, all of the hunters scattered—but not before Tamsin heard a cacophony of bullets that sent panicked birds flying from the forest.

Then silence.

Three black sedans roared up on the road. One kept going in pursuit of the van while the other two parked at the edge of the forest grove.

"*Patrón!*" Reyes shouted.

Marcos shouted back a reply. Overcome with relief, Tamsin sagged against him. He put his arm around her, supporting her.

"I'm sorry," she whispered. "I'm sorry. I didn't want you to be hurt. I didn't want to leave you in the middle of the night. But my sister…"

"It's all right," he said softly. "It's all right now, *querida*."

Suddenly, her whole body hurt and the cut on her foot screamed with pain. She stumbled as he led her out of the forest. Without a word, he picked her up in his arms, cradling her close to his body as he carried her back to the road.

She was too exhausted to protest. Too grateful. All she could think was that they were both alive, and she was in Marcos's arms. He'd risked death for her.

His beautiful red Ferrari had been left riddled with bullet holes. Aziz hadn't been able to get Tamsin or

Marcos, so he'd taken out his frustration on the expensive car. Utterly destroyed, smoke rose from its crushed hood like a pallid ghost.

Marcos's hands tightened, but his face showed no reaction. For Tamsin, it was the last straw.

Aziz was a horrible, cruel man. Marcos was right. He would never have let her go. But, if she didn't marry him, what could she do? What could she possibly do to save her sister?

She pressed her face against Marcos's chest as sudden sobs racked her body.

As she cried, she felt his whole body go tense. He started shouting out orders and, a moment later, she was in the back seat of the sedan, still cradled in his arms. Within moments, he'd whisked her back to the castle.

Without a word, he deposited her into her guest room and left. As a maid drew her bath, Tamsin's tears dried up. She put on a fresh nightgown and, by the time the doctor arrived to bandage her foot, she felt numb again. The maid brought some tea and buttered toast and tucked her into bed.

As comfortable as the bed was, Tamsin's whole body cried out to be back in Marcos's bedroom, to be in his arms—the only place she'd felt safe. But why would he want her now? She'd tricked him, run away, nearly gotten him killed and finally sobbed all over his shirt. No wonder he'd just left her.

In spite of spending the previous night lost, wandering around in circles across the dark Spanish countryside, she didn't expect to sleep. But within two minutes she did. She didn't wake up until hours later, when long afternoon shadows were spilling across the tiles of her bedroom floor. She blinked, feeling groggy, wondering what the doctor had slipped into her tea.

"Feeling better?"

Marcos was sitting in a chair near the fire, watching her. She wondered how long he'd been there.

"Yes." Surprisingly, it was the truth. Then she remembered Nicole and sat up in bed. "But my sister is still with Sheldon and Camilla! I don't know what they'll do to her if I don't—"

"We will save her."

"How?" she asked, touched in spite of herself by his unexpected use of 'we'. "My brother will never let her go. Not while she has money in her trust fund."

"I won't let him hurt either of you," he said. "I didn't have my investigators focus on the child. That was my mistake. If I'd been more thorough, I would have known what Sheldon was doing." His jaw clenched. "I'll get provable evidence of your brother's neglect and thievery and we'll file a petition for custody."

"But I told you. There's no way I'll get custody of Nicole. Everyone in Britain thinks I'm a flighty, promiscuous little tart." She gave him a tight smile. "Just like you did."

"I don't think that of you any more." His eyes met hers. "And no one will think that of my wife."

What kind of drugs had the doctor given her, anyway?

She licked her dry lips. "I'm sorry, I think I'm hallucinating. Did you just ask me to be your wife?"

He abruptly rose from the chair and sat down next to her on the bed. "What if I did?"

His proximity made her nervous. She moved her hand away from his on the blanket. "You don't love me, for one thing!"

"Why is that a problem? Do you love me?"

Her heart did a painful flip at his question. Of course she didn't love him. It was true she'd given him her virginity, and he'd made love to her in a way she could still feel all over her body. She hadn't wanted to leave him, and then he'd saved her life in the forest and she'd felt…something.

But it wasn't love, she assured herself. She wouldn't be that stupid.

"No," she said finally. "Of course I don't love you."

"You didn't love Aziz either, but you couldn't wait to marry him." He gave her a grim smile. "I promise I'll be a better husband than Aziz. For one thing, I will give you a speedy divorce. It will be a marriage of convenience between us. Just long enough to get you custody of your sister."

She swallowed, wanting to ask if his proposal meant he'd forgiven her for tricking him and escaping through the tunnel. Looking up into his eyes, she didn't have the courage. She murmured, "Why are you going out of your way to help me?"

He stood up abruptly. "Because I had a brother."

"Had?" she asked timidly.

"He died," he said.

"I'm so sorry. How—"

"I don't want to discuss it."

His voice was brittle, brusque. She wanted to know more, but could see by the hard, tense lines of his body that asking questions would be a waste of time.

Was it possible that his brother's death was somehow linked to Marcos's desire for revenge?

Impossible, she thought. Aziz might be a murderer, but her brother was not. He was a weak buffoon with poor taste in women, not a murderer of children.

Although he had abandoned Nicole to starve…

She shook the image out of her head. She would get custody of her sister soon and then she'd always be safe. They both would. Thanks to Marcos.

She looked up at him. "Whatever your motives for helping me, thank you," she said softly. "That you'd give up your revenge in order to help me save Nicole…"

"Give it up?" His dark eyebrows lowered. "I've been planning it for twenty years. I'm not giving up my revenge for you or anyone."

Twenty years? Marcos couldn't be older than thirty-two or thirty-three. He'd been plotting against Aziz and her half-brother since he'd been just a boy?

What on earth had they done?

"In fact…" Marcos went to the window, looking out at the wide expanse of his lands. When he turned back, his eyes were hard and his smile was chilling. "Taking you as my bride will play nicely into my plans. It will humiliate Aziz, making him look like a fool to the world. And it will show Sheldon that I have control over not just him, but his whole family."

The chill from his smile spread across Tamsin's heart.

Thank God I don't love him, she thought. *What kind of man could take a good deed and turn it so black?*

Pushing her blanket aside, she climbed out of bed. "I need to dress."

The light in his eyes changed as he came closer to her. "Let me help you."

He ran his hands down her arms, and the heat in his eyes made her forget her earlier chill. He made her forget that she was wearing a long cotton nightgown that covered her from her neck to her toes. He made her feel naked. Naked and on fire.

"I thought you said that…that our marriage would be in name only," she stammered.

"I never said that, *querida*." He gave her a slow once-over that made her whole body sizzle. "I said it would be a marriage of convenience. And it will be very convenient for me to have you sleeping in the same bed every night. Very convenient to have you naked next to me, instead of wearing the shapeless, chaste nightgowns that you favor. You cannot hide your body from me. I will not allow it. What I've tasted has only made me hungry for more."

He ran his hands down her back, pulling her close. Her heart started to pound and she felt frightened—of him, of herself and what he made her feel. How could such a cold-hearted man make her feel so…hot?

She twisted out of his reach with a nervous laugh, reaching for a plush robe inside her closet. "I'm starving."

His eyes smoldered. "So am I."

She swallowed, aware of the bed right behind her, of how easy it would be to surrender. But she had to resist. Making love to him made her feel things she didn't want to feel—things she couldn't let herself feel. If they were going to be married for months, she couldn't let herself fall in love with him. To keep her heart distant, she had to do the same with her body.

"I meant for food." She covered her nightgown with the thick white robe and double-tied the belt. "Can you point me towards the kitchen?"

"I'll do better than that." He gave her a wolflike smile. "I will show you personally."

"No, there's no need to do that, really. I'm sure I can find—"

"I will take you." The way he spoke the words made her shiver. He intended to take her—and not just to the kitchen, either. But surely he wouldn't try to seduce her in a place so public as his kitchen, in the middle of the afternoon? She took a steadying breath.

"All right."

He grabbed her hand in his own larger one and drew her out of the bedroom and down the sweeping stairs. They descended several floors to the enormous kitchen tucked in the far back of the castle. The ancient brick oven, wood beams across the low ceiling and wood panels on the walls gave the kitchen a medieval appearance that contrasted with the bright stainless steel appliances and modern amenities.

"Here we are," he said softly.

They were as alone as they'd been in her room. She swallowed.

"Where is everyone? I thought the kitchen would be crowded with servants making dinner."

"Sorry to disappoint you, but it's siesta. Dinner is not for many hours." He quirked an eyebrow. "Are you afraid to be alone with me, Señorita Winter?"

"No, of course not," she lied. "I just want a sandwich and, from what your housekeeper said, you couldn't find your way around a kitchen if your life depended on it."

He quirked an eyebrow. "You have so little faith in me."

Her blood rose in spite of her best intentions. Sparring with this cocky, arrogant Spaniard thrilled her. He so richly deserved to be set down a peg or two. Raising her chin, she shrugged. "Every man has his weaknesses."

"This is not one of mine, *querida*. I rarely pay attention to food, simply because it doesn't interest me. But feeding you…that interests me very much."

He was already grabbing things from the refrigerator and the cupboards. Serrano ham, cheese, Dijon mustard, lettuce, tomatoes and thick crusty bread.

"What are you doing?"

He assembled the ingredients into a sandwich that looked five inches tall.

"Sit down," he ordered. She sat at the small round table and he sat across from her, handing her the tall sandwich on a plate. "Try this."

"There's no way I can eat that!" she protested. "My mouth isn't wide enough."

He gave her a wicked grin. "I think you can handle it."

Her stomach growled just looking at the sandwich. Feeling awkward, she stretched her mouth to take a bite and her whole body sang with pleasure at the taste. She'd never known ham could be so delicious. "It's wonderful," she exclaimed, wiping a trace of mustard from the corner of her mouth.

He gave her a condescending smile. "So you admit it, then. Making a sandwich is not one of my weaknesses."

"No," she had to admit. She took another bite, and

another, before she noticed that he was still motionless, watching her from the other side of the table. "Aren't you going to have one?"

"I'm saving my appetite," he said. "For dessert."

"Oh." She took another bite, and then realized what he meant. "Oh."

His smile widened as if he'd read her thoughts. "Ice cream," he clarified.

Perversely, she felt disappointed. The more she ate, the stronger she felt. She was already thinking that maybe physical contact wouldn't be so dangerous after all. She knew Marcos was cold and vengeful, and that it would be a disaster to love him, but she was now feeling confident that she could handle it.

Making love might make other women fall in love, but not her. She could resist.

She looked down at her empty plate with surprise. "I ate the whole thing."

"Of course you did." He reached across the table to stroke her cheek. "You're not one of those sickly women who exist on lettuce leaves and diet soda. You are too much of a fighter. Too much in love with life and all the pleasure that comes with it."

She turned her face into his caress, and his eyes sharpened. He leaned across the table—moving slowly, so slowly—and kissed her thoroughly. She closed her eyes, never wanting it to end. He pulled her to her feet and untied her robe, pulling it off her shoulders and dropping it to the floor. Her nightgown, modest as it was, felt thin as gossamer between them.

"Do you want some dessert?" he whispered, his lips brushing against hers.

Eyes still closed, she felt breathless and giddy. Her earlier fears and hesitations now seemed foolish. Marcos had called her a fighter. He believed she was strong. Why should she deny herself the pleasure of making love because of some ridiculous fear that she might lose her heart?

And, anyway, they'd already made love once. Once more wouldn't hurt, surely?

"Yes," she said, as soft as a sigh. "Dessert."

He released her. Crossing the kitchen, he pulled two cartons of ice cream from the freezer. "Chocolate or strawberry?"

"What?" she stammered.

"Ice cream." He waved the cartons at her. "You said you wanted some."

"Oh," she said, disappointed. "Either one."

"I think both." He put the cartons down on the large stone slab of the center island in the kitchen. His dark eyes seared hers as he held out his hand. "Come."

Mesmerized by the intensity in his expression, she put her hand in his. Without explanation, he bent in front of her and, in a single upwards motion, pulled off her nightgown.

"What are you doing?" she gasped, trying to cover her naked breasts with her arms. They were in a public place! At any moment one of his servants, like Reyes or even that ghastly housekeeper Nelida, could walk in and see her like this! "We can't—"

"I can." Without any apparent effort, he picked her up and laid her across the cool stone of the center island. Ignoring her struggles, he left her bare on the table, wearing only white cotton panties. He stood over her.

"And now," he said, "dessert."

He dipped a spoon into the gourmet chocolate ice cream. "Open your mouth."

Shocked, she stopped struggling long enough to let her lips fall open slightly. But he didn't put the spoon in her mouth. Instead, he ran the back of it along her lips in an explosion of cold, rich flavor. It tasted good, so good.

She involuntarily licked her lips. "More?" she suggested in a small voice.

"Yes." But, instead of giving her another taste of ice cream, he leaned over and kissed her. The sudden heat from his mouth and the long, languid strokes of his tongue caused a shock of desire to spread across her body. She forgot that she was practically naked in the kitchen and didn't care who might see. She just wanted Marcos to be naked too.

She reached for him. "Kiss me."

He kissed her, but it was only a light teasing kiss that just made her want more. He dipped his spoon into the strawberry ice cream. He ran the back of the spoon around her breast, swirling it in increasingly tightening circles until it reached her nipple. He turned the spoon over, leaving a mouthful of strawberry ice cream against her taut flesh, then bent and sucked it off her nipple.

She gasped, arching her back against the cool stone. Pulling away, he did the same thing to her other breast, and she thought she'd go mad.

"Please," she whimpered, pulling at his shirt, fumbling at his buttons. "Don't make me wait."

"You want me to take off my clothes?"

She nodded.

Raising a dark eyebrow, he gave her a wicked smile. "But you're covered in ice cream. In the kitchen. Anyone might walk in and see."

So it was like that, was it? Narrowing her eyes, she sat up. If she could be nearly naked and risk discovery, so could he. She yanked off his shirt, ripping off two buttons in her impatience, and covered herself with it. His shirt barely reached the tops of her thighs, and the one remaining button was inadequate protection for her breasts, but it was enough. Leaving the two pints of ice cream melting on the counter, she grabbed his hand and pulled him out of the kitchen.

"Señor," she heard the housekeeper say behind them as they reached the first floor landing, "I was just going to start dinner and wondered if you'd prefer *langostinos* or *rabo de toro*…" She ended with a gasp.

Tamsin whirled around to face the housekeeper, well aware of the woman's pinched face and judgmental sniff at her wearing nothing but Marcos's shirt. But, for once, she didn't care.

"We'll have the *langostinos*," Tamsin said. With a toss of her hair, she added, "Just don't make it too soon. Marcos and I will be busy for hours."

Then she turned back to the stairs, pulling Marcos behind her and leaving Nelida spluttering in Spanish outrage.

"You've changed," he observed as she dragged him into her bedroom. She looked at him quickly, wondering if he was criticizing her. But his dark eyes were full of approval.

She tilted her head, putting her hand on her hip. "Ice cream will do that to a girl."

"A dangerous dish," he agreed, then his eyes widened as she deliberately pulled off the shirt and dropped it to the floor. As he watched, she leaned back, closing her bedroom door behind her. He licked his lips, seemingly mesmerized as she pulled off her panties. "Yes, very dangerous," he repeated. "It should be a controlled substance."

"I thought you controlled it remarkably well." She was naked in front of a man in broad daylight. The old Tamsin would have been running for a blanket to cover herself. But somehow at this moment she didn't even care. She felt saucy, bold—and utterly unafraid. It was exhilarating.

She grabbed his belt loop. "Come with me."

He didn't even try to resist. "Where?"

She pulled him into her bathroom. It had a wide walk-in shower enclosed in Spanish tile, with two nozzles on opposite sides. The temperature of the water was controlled by digital settings. Turning on the water, she set it to a steamy forty-one degrees centigrade.

Stepping back out of the shower, she knelt in front of him and pulled off his pants and boxers. He was already hard. She stared at him for a moment. She'd never really looked at any man up close like this. He was beautiful.

Tentatively, she touched him.

He almost jumped out of his skin.

She looked up at his tense face. So he wasn't the only one who could be a tease, she thought. He wasn't the only one who could make a person die from wanting more.

The thought was illuminating—and satisfying. She

ran her breasts against his bare legs. Moving her hand between his thighs, exploring the length of his shaft, she leaned forward and took a soft lick. Salty, she thought. Smooth.

"*Dios mío*," he muttered, taking an involuntary, stumbling step towards her.

Reveling in her own power, she took a wide, long taste of him, like licking an ice cream cone. He trembled beneath her and, with a harsh gasp, he swept her up into his arms.

"You little tease," he growled, and he carried her into the shower, pushing her against the colorful tile wall. Hot water steamed all around them, twisting her hair and drenching her skin.

"Turnabout's fair play," she gasped.

"You deserve this, then." He lifted her up against the wall, forcing her thighs apart as he spread her wide. Her legs wrapped around him. Holding her up against the wall as if she were no weight at all, he pushed himself inside her.

The shock of his penetration made her cry out. Her whole body was massaged with hot water as he thrust into her again possessively. She threw her head back, closing her eyes as her breasts swayed with each thrust. She came almost at once, crying out, and he followed immediately with a shout that echoed against the tiles of the shower.

For a moment, he just held her against the wall, his head lowered, his cheek against hers. Water continued to pound them, leaving their skin flushed.

Finally, he set her down. Her legs felt too weak to support her and she fell against his hard, muscled chest.

He led her out of the shower and toweled them both off. Stroking her cheek, he looked down at her almost tenderly.

Then, suddenly, a change came over his face.

"What's wrong?"

He shook his head, clenching his jaw. Pulling on his pants, he went out into the bedroom. Still naked, she followed him.

"What is it?"

"Nothing," he said.

She sat down on the bed. She wanted to invite him under the sheets with her, but his face was as hard and set as granite. "Tell me."

He started for the door, then stopped, glaring at her. "It's not you," he muttered. "It's what you do to me. You made me lose control. I've never done that before, Tamsin. Ever."

"Done what? Eaten ice cream? Or made love in the shower?" She blushed a little. "That was my first time as well. I have a new appreciation for it."

She expected him to smile, but his eyes looked grimmer by the second. "We will leave for Madrid tonight."

"Madrid? Why not London?"

"I will never set foot in that city again," he said flatly. "I made a vow when I was twelve, and I never go back on my word."

She licked her lips. Just five minutes before, he'd been toweling her off in the gorgeous bathroom, brushing every drop of moisture off her skin with a white cotton towel. His face had been caring, almost adoring. Now he was staring at her as if he hated her.

"But Marcos, the custody hearing will be in Britain,"

she pointed out, confused. "And you said yourself that's where we need to change public opinion of me…"

"No." Abruptly, he walked away and she felt a rush of cold and solitude. His sudden emotional abandonment felt like a physical pain. He was punishing her. She didn't know why, but it hurt. In a daze, she pulled the blankets up over her naked body. She no longer felt saucy or bold. She just felt vulnerable.

"We'll give the press a week in Madrid to document our whirlwind affair," he continued. "Then we'll be married in a fairy tale wedding. The English press will pick up the story. All of London will be sighing over our *romance*."

His emphasis on the last word was almost a sneer. Her pride began to react.

"The marriage might not be necessary," she retorted. "If your detectives find enough evidence against my brother, we can use the information to pressure him into giving us custody."

"I said I'd marry you, and that's what I intend to do."

"Maybe I no longer want to marry you."

His gray eyes flashed. "What the hell is that supposed to mean?"

"What's wrong with you? Why are you so angry at me? What did I do?"

Clenching his jaw, he raked his hand through his dark hair. "I told you, it wasn't you."

"Then why are you acting like you hate me?"

"I didn't use a condom, Tamsin," he bit out. "I've never forgotten to use one. Ever. I've never lost control like that." He ground his teeth, "You could be pregnant already."

"Oh," she said in a small voice. Pregnant. Oh, God. How could she have forgotten about that? How could she have not noticed that they didn't use a condom in the shower?

He gave a harsh laugh. "Don't look so frightened."

"I'm not. I'm sure everything will be fine," she said desperately. "We just forgot the condom once."

"That's all it takes."

"But it seems pretty unlikely that we are…that we could be…that anything could happen," she finished lamely.

She tried to act unconcerned, but inside she was terrified. Marrying Marcos was bad enough, but having his baby? That would be almost worse than marrying Aziz. Because Marcos affected her in ways that Aziz never could.

He tempted her to love him, even knowing the darkness of his soul. He could drag her down into a shadowy world of mixed-up anguish and desire from which she might never emerge.

"I wasn't made to be a father, do you understand?" he said fiercely. "You can't be pregnant. It can't happen."

She blinked at him, reaching for his hand. "It's unlikely I'll fall pregnant but, if it happens, we'll deal with it."

"Right," he muttered. He endured her touch for one second, then dropped her hand. "Let's go. The servants will pack for us. Tonight we'll sleep in Madrid and by next week we'll be married. You'll make an honest man of me at last." He gave her an ironic smile. "Shall we go tell Nelida the good news?"

I just won't love him, she told herself as she followed him out of the room. She'd only stay married to him for as long as it took to gain custody of Nicole. She didn't know why he was so afraid to become a father, but everything would be fine. She couldn't be pregnant, not after just one time.

She could make the paparazzi believe they were in love without actually loving him. She could enjoy his company every day and make love to him every night without giving him her heart.

But part of her worried that it was already too late.

CHAPTER SIX

MARCOS had lived in Madrid for years, but being with
Tamsin made the experience entirely new. Five days
with her felt more vibrant and alive than the five years
he'd lived there before.

Era verdad, in the past he'd spent most of his time
there working. He'd kept in shape and worked off stress
at a local fight club; he'd occasionally gone out for a
tapeo with friends, or met a woman at a club and taken
her home. Easy. No strings. He'd liked it that way. For
most of his life, he'd kept himself tightly in control,
focusing all of his energy on building his fortune and
planning his revenge.

But being with Tamsin changed everything.

She made him lose control. She made him feel like
a wild, impetuous boy again, following his pleasures
and impulses without thinking of the cost.

He didn't like it.

He couldn't resist it.

It was bad enough that she'd made him trust her. Bad
enough that he'd slept in her arms and gloried in being
the first man who'd ever made love to her. Since then,
they'd made love so many times that he'd lost count.

JENNIE LUCAS   117

She made him feel. Believe. Dream of a life he'd long ago given up as a fantasy.

But if she should be pregnant…

It couldn't happen. Every life he touched, he ruined. Everyone he'd ever loved had died.

He couldn't have another family. He couldn't risk loving a wife. He couldn't risk having a child.

But he'd been wrong to take out his anger on Tamsin at the castle. It wasn't her fault she had such an effect on him. It wasn't her fault that even when his mind hadn't been sure he could trust her, his body had.

Since that one time in the shower, he and Tamsin had been careful to use protection. For the last five days, they'd focused on making a splash, attracting the attention of the paparazzi and making the whole world believe that they were wildly in love.

They'd gone motorcycle racing through the traffic of the Gran Via, then boating in the Casa de Campo. They'd rocked out to a late-night concert at Suristán one night, and had box seats for classical Spanish theater at the Teatro Pavón the next. He'd taken her to a dance club on the Calle Orense where they'd drunk *mojitos* and danced all night. At a sultry flamenco bar on the Calle de Echegaray, he'd been so mesmerized by the red lanterns against Tamsin's pale skin and the way Tamsin had unconsciously swayed with the music, he'd watched her instead of the dancers.

As he'd anticipated, the paparazzi had followed them, intrigued by the affair between the well-known Spanish millionaire and the young British cosmetics heiress. They always had bodyguards, of course. Marcos wasn't taking any chances that Aziz might descend upon them with greater numbers and attempt to take Tamsin by force.

He'd never phoned Aziz or Sheldon. He hadn't needed to. Each photo of Marcos and Tamsin broadcast around the world told his enemies all they needed to know, humiliating them both.

But Marcos's focus had been on Tamsin. He would enjoy her, get her custody of her sister, and then send her on her way. Their time together would be short. It had to be. He couldn't risk loving her or, worse— having her fall in love with him.

He couldn't stay out of control like this for ever.

But, so far, everything was going as he'd planned. Every day, pictures of them appeared in the papers with greater prominence and, since they'd announced their engagement two days ago, they'd started to appear in the British tabloids as well.

His particular favorite was the photo that had appeared yesterday, of Marcos helping Tamsin get into a taxi at dawn on the *Calle Orense*. She'd had mussed hair and a wrinkled cocktail dress; he'd had a bruise on his neck.

He smiled to himself, remembering. She'd been so beautiful he hadn't been able to resist kissing her on the dance floor. The kiss had lasted until he couldn't take it any longer and he'd taken her to an empty room in the club's basement. Surrounded by crates of champagne and boxes of liquor bottles, he'd pulled up her short red skirt and taken her roughly against the concrete wall. He still remembered the way she'd gasped and trembled beneath him, sucking on his neck, coming almost at once.

He really needed to take her out dancing more, he thought. Perhaps tonight.

Somehow, over the last five days, he'd actually had moments where he'd forgotten entirely about his revenge and just felt…happy. It made him uneasy. This morning, going to his ten-story office building on the Paseo de la Castellana for the first time in a week, he'd actually caught himself whistling. He'd meant to stay at work for a half day, but within an hour he found himself distracted by thoughts of Tamsin. In bed. Against the wall. On the table. Everywhere.

He eyed his large cherrywood desk with interest. If Tamsin had come into work with him today, he'd have had no problem with wanting to stay. But as it was…

Closing his laptop, he told his two assistants to take the rest of the day off.

"In love," he heard his executive secretary whisper behind him.

"Definitely," his second assistant replied.

He turned around with a scowl. "On second thought…" He waited until they looked apprehensive, then he finished, "Take the rest of the week off."

"Tomorrow as well?" his secretary gasped. "What about the KDL hedge fund? And the Tokyo investments are so volatile—"

"You can't be serious, *señor*. What about the merger? The New York office—"

"It'll all sort itself out," he replied, and gave them a grin. "I'm going to Jávia."

Three whole days with Tamsin in a charming beach town on the Costa Blanca. He could hardly wait. He wondered if they'd even leave their rented villa long enough to walk the beach.

If that anticipation wasn't enough, the startled look

his employees gave him was priceless. They acted as if they didn't even recognize him. Well, maybe he had been behaving a little different lately, but who could blame him? He'd never had reason to focus solely on his own enjoyment, or had a lover who made it so irresistible.

Whistling a few notes of a *canción de flamenco*, he crossed the wide, busy office floor of Ramirez Ibérica S.R.L. and pressed the button on the elevator. He wondered what Tamsin was packing into her suitcase right at that instant. Nothing, he hoped. Nothing always looked good on her.

The elevator doors opened with a ding. Inside, he saw four hulking men in turbans and ankle-length *jellaba* robes. Between them an elderly man with skin the color of walnuts stared at him with bright, beady eyes.

The office noise behind him faded as Marcos recognized Sheikh Mohamed ibn Battuta al-Maghrib. Aziz's uncle was honored, powerful and wealthy beyond belief. He was also proficient at making people disappear.

Marcos's mood instantly sobered. He stepped into the elevator and felt the doors close behind him.

"You have something that belongs to my family," the Sheikh said pleasantly in Oxford-accented English.

Scanning the bodyguards, trying to estimate weight class and his best strategy if they should attack, Marcos tightened his hands around the handle of his laptop bag, preparing to use it as a weapon if necessary. "She was being forced into the marriage against her will."

"And what claim do you have on her? My nephew

is screaming for your blood, as is my niece Hatima, who is angry about the kidnapping. They say vengeance is a matter of family honor."

"Aziz al-Maghrib has no right to speak of honor. He is a murderer and a thief."

The older man's eyes widened. "You speak this insult to my face?"

"It is the truth."

The heavy-lidded eyes looked at him evenly, with something approaching respect. "Bold words. Can you prove them?"

Clenching his jaw, Marcos shook his head.

Scanning his face, the Sheikh narrowed his eyes, then gave a swift nod. "*Bixir*. If your claim is true, you will have your justice. You have three days to prove your claim. My nephew will not attack you, nor try to take his bride by force. I will hold him back for three days, and then you will present your proof."

"And if I don't?" Marcos asked sharply.

The Sheikh gave an eloquent shrug, but his face was sharp. "Then you'll have more than just my nephew to worry about."

Tamsin stared out of the wide expanse of windows. Marcos's penthouse included the entire top floor of the elegant art-deco building. Wearing her robe, she walked out on the wraparound balcony, holding her coffee in the cool pink dawn. In the distance, she could see two tall glass towers on opposite sides of the wide street, stretching over the busy traffic toward each other in a triangular point. Marcos had told her they were called the Torres Kio, or the Gate of Europe.

She and Marcos were like that, she thought suddenly. Reaching towards each other, but not able to touch. Too much separated them.

His elegant penthouse, with its incredible views down the Paseo de la Castellana and the financial district of eastern Madrid, felt strangely empty. Marcos had left suddenly the night before, canceling their beach vacation, refusing to tell her where he was going or why. And, without him, this place that had been full of so much delight now just felt lonely.

Lonely—that was a laugh. Marcos had left a six-man security detail led by Reyes in the flat beneath hers. They kept watch over the building to prevent Aziz, the paparazzi or any celebrity gawkers from getting too close, and frequently contacted her to ensure she was comfortable and safe. Tamsin felt as if she were a child left with minders, but Marcos had been intractable.

She'd missed him in bed last night.

She took a sip of the strong Spanish coffee. She'd made it herself that morning in Marcos's immaculate white kitchen that looked like it had never been used. Three different bodyguards had offered to fetch her coffee from a shop, but really, enough was enough. She might have to endure a squadron of bodyguards, but she could make her own coffee.

But should she even be drinking it?

Could she be pregnant? At twenty-three, she felt totally unready to be a mother. Having a child with a man who didn't love her wasn't exactly her domestic fantasy; having a child with a man who didn't even want one would be a disaster.

But why was Marcos so afraid of becoming a father?

She took another sip, staring out at the city. Her own father should never have had children. He'd been so focused on revenging petty slights that he'd hurt everyone stupid enough to love him. He hadn't even been with her mother when she'd died. He'd been down the hall, screaming curses at the hospital administrator over some imagined insult from a doctor.

And so her mother had died alone. Without Tamsin, who had believed her mother to be in remission and so had remained at boarding school for final exams. And she'd died without Nicole, who at two years old had been at home with Nanny, crying for the mother she hadn't seen in days.

When her father had finally called Tamsin to tell her of her mother's death, he'd barely mentioned the lovely, glowing woman she'd been. He certainly hadn't said a word about loving her. Instead, he'd spent ten minutes screaming about the doctor and the administrator and promising to sue them all. As if it was somehow their fault. As if it would bring their mother back.

And Marcos was just the same. Another man bent on revenge who didn't care who he hurt.

A shiver went through her and she clutched at her thin silk robe in the early-morning cool.

She was the one who should be frightened of pregnancy. Because Marcos Ramirez was the kind of man she'd always sworn to avoid. Dangerous, delicious, exciting—yes. But as a husband? As a father?

She'd always wondered how her father had convinced three different women over his lifetime to love him. Now she thought she knew.

She placed her hand on her belly. She couldn't be pregnant. She prayed she wasn't. Not with Marcos's baby. It would already be too easy to love him. Terrifyingly easy.

And she could not commit herself to a man who coldly placed revenge above everything, even his own family. She couldn't let another innocent child be hurt like she and Nicole and even Sheldon had been.

She went back into the flat and got dressed with care. Putting on her mascara in the bathroom, she blinked at herself in the mirror.

It should have been a happy day: she was going to pick out her wedding dress. But, instead, she had a heavy heart and dark circles under her eyes.

She turned right and left, frowning. The under-eye concealer hadn't worked at all. A pity she didn't have the Winter Anti-Aging ConcealStick with her. It was her favorite product, but Winter cosmetics were becoming harder to find abroad. Poor brand management, she thought, shaking her head with a scowl. If she'd been a boy, maybe her father would have let her run the company instead of Sheldon.

But, of course, if she'd been a boy, maybe she wouldn't have cared about concealer.

She'd just have to manage without it. It was her second time that month as a bride, and neither had been anything like her girlish dreams. All her life, she'd thought she would marry for love.

I don't need love, she told herself, pinching her cheeks savagely for color. She liked Marcos. She enjoyed their time together in bed. And, most importantly, marrying him would help her gain custody of Nicole.

That was all that mattered. Not love. Love was for dreams, not reality.

In fact, she thanked her lucky stars she wasn't in love with Marcos. What a horrible disaster that would have been.

"Find a dress tomorrow," he'd told her before he left. "Pick your favorite and the designer will get it to you in time for our wedding. Even if their assistants work around the clock." His eyes had glinted wickedly. "I'll have fun taking the dress off you."

As long as she wasn't pregnant, marrying him wouldn't be so bad, she told herself as she got in the elevator. They would have their wedding night. And since they'd arrived in Madrid, every moment she'd spent with Marcos had felt like a holiday. Even when he made her furious, being with him somehow made her…happy.

The September sun felt warm against her crisp Chanel suit and wide-brimmed black hat as she stepped outside. Photographers screamed her name, trying to get her to look towards their cameras as Reyes and another bodyguard escorted her to the waiting Rolls-Royce. She fell back in the seat as the chauffeur drove smoothly away on the Castellana.

Another wedding, another limo, she thought, remembering Tarfaya. Things had changed, she thought, staring out at the busy Madrid street. She suddenly gasped.

"Stop!" she screamed. "Please stop!"

The chauffeur pulled over with a screech of brakes. Reyes, who was in the front seat, put his hand on his gun as he leapt out of the car. The two young women who'd been waving at her furiously from the sidewalk jumped back in fear before Tamsin could explain. A moment later, just as they were starting to attract attention from the paparazzi half a block away, the three girls were talking excitedly in the back seat as the Rolls-Royce pulled back into the traffic.

"Finally!" Bianca said, bouncing up and down on her seat. "We've been here since yesterday. We read about you in London and had to come. We tried to call, but your old cellphone didn't work. We went to see you but, every time we tried to visit, one of your bouncers stopped us. This guy you're marrying, is he the richest man in the world or what? I mean, a bodyguard is one thing, but do you really need a whole army?"

"Is it true, Tamsin?" Daisy interrupted. "You're marrying Marcos Ramirez?"

"It's true," Tamsin said, smiling through the tears. Seeing Bianca and Daisy, her best friends since boarding school days, was overwhelming. "My wedding to Aziz was canceled."

The other girls cheered.

"Oh, I'm so glad," Bianca said, giving her a hug.

But Daisy frowned. "Another quickie wedding? This isn't some new scheme from your brother and that wretched wife of his, is it? Though it's hard for me to imagine. Your Spaniard looks delicious in the photos."

"Yeah." Bianca sighed. "I wish someone would force me to marry a man like that."

"He's even more handsome in person," Tamsin said. "No, Sheldon had nothing to do with it. It was all Marcos's idea. Can you stay for the wedding? It's in two days."

"I wish," Bianca said wistfully. "But I have to be

back in London by tonight, and Daisy leaves for New York in four hours."

"You both have to leave Madrid tonight?" Tamsin's heart plummeted. "You can't stay two more days?"

"I wish I could," Daisy said regretfully. "But my new job starts tomorrow. I'm going to be jet-lagged as it is."

"And Michaelmas term starts early for molecular biology," said Bianca, looking glum. "The prep time alone is harder than I thought it would be."

Tamsin forced a cheerful smile. "Well, then, we'll just have a nice chat this afternoon. Tell me about your new job, Daiz, and all about Oxford, Bianca. And you can help me pick out my wedding dress!"

"Wedding dress!" Bianca squealed so loudly that Tamsin, laughing, covered her ears. Of the three friends, Bianca was by far the most romantic. As the youngest daughter of a wealthy Italian-American family, she'd been protected and cosseted her whole life, but her idealistic outlook and kind heart were reflected in her expressive black eyes.

"Your wedding dress!" she repeated. "Oh, yes! Please! I might never get a chance to pick one for myself. I'll soon be one of those spinster professors you hear about. And you know Daisy, she'll never trust a man enough to marry him. So you have to let us live vicariously through you. You have to!"

Blinking back tears, Tamsin nodded, realizing she wouldn't have to pick out her dress alone after all. "Thank you for coming to find me."

"I didn't exactly have a choice." Daisy, who'd had a far more difficult childhood than Bianca and had never owned a pair of rose-colored glasses in her life, leaned back against the leather seat. "Bianca insisted on coming to Madrid, and I figured I'd better come along to make sure she didn't lose her purse, her passport and her virtue to the first smooth-talking Spaniard she met."

Bianca started to protest and all three women were laughing by the time they arrived at the bridal designer's *atelier*. Once they arrived, Reyes remained at the front to guard the door while they were whisked inside and seated on an ultra-plush sofa for their private appointment. Assistants brought them champagne, sandwiches and strawberries dipped in chocolate while models showed them a selection of dresses. An hour later, they were on their second bottle of champagne, and Tamsin was having a wonderful time.

"That one," Daisy said with a loud snicker, pointing at the ugliest, poofiest one covered with the most bows. Even the model looked embarrassed to be wearing it.

"No, that one," Bianca said dreamily, gazing at a sleek shift in white satin, worn by a model with hair black as her own covered by a long gauzy veil.

But Tamsin knew her dress the instant she saw it. She said in Spanish to the designer, "I'd like to try that one please, *señora*."

Her friends gasped when she came out of the dressing room a few minutes later.

"Oh, Tamsin," Bianca whispered, tears in her eyes. "You look like an angel."

"Not bad," Daisy said approvingly.

Tamsin looked at herself in the three-way mirror and caught her breath. At last, something was exactly just the way she'd dreamed it would be as a girl.

The strapless white ball gown had a sweetheart neckline, a tight corset waist and voluminous skirts with embroidered French silk draped over an ocean of tulle. With the slender tiara of diamonds and veil, she looked like a princess from a fairy tale.

She knew immediately that she was not leaving the designer's shop without this dress.

"You even fit into the sample size. Maybe they'll give you a discount."

"I don't need a discount, Daiz," Tamsin said absently, still staring at herself in the mirror.

Daisy lifted a skeptical eyebrow. "Last I heard, you'd lost your trust fund."

"That's not a problem any more." Tamsin moved from side to side, watching the way the light danced off the voluminous fabric of her skirts. "Marcos has more money than he can spend."

Her friend paused. "But that's not why you're marrying him, right?"

"Of course it's not!" Bianca protested loyally. "She's marrying him for the only good reason you marry anyone."

Daisy tilted her head at Tamsin, frowning. "You're pregnant?"

"No!" she replied, rolling her eyes. "I'm not pregnant." At least, she hoped she wasn't. Maybe she'd better say it again, just to make sure the universe was listening. "I'm definitely not pregnant. And I don't care about his money. I'm marrying him because…"

Because I need to get custody of my sister, she intended to say. But as she opened her mouth to speak the words, a barrage of images went through her mind.

Of Marcos kissing her on the dance floor of the club on the Calle Orense. Of the boyish, dreaming expression on his face while he slept. The hard look in his eyes when he offered to die for her in the forest. His wild shout of laughter when she'd gunned her motorcycle to pass him on the Gran Via.

Marcos fierce, Marcos angry, Marcos laughing. The sensual look in his eyes when he pulled her into his arms, first thing in the morning, and kissed her until she thought she'd die of joy.

Tamsin sat down abruptly in a *phoof* of tulle and French silk. "…Because I love him," she said slowly. "Oh, my God. I love him."

"Of course you do," Bianca said comfortingly.

But Daisy's eyes met her own. "What's wrong, Tamsin?"

Tamsin put her face in her hands. "It was supposed to be a marriage of convenience," she whispered. "But I've fallen for him. I can't believe I'm so stupid."

In a sharp movement, Daisy turned to the designer's two assistants, still hovering near the door. "Go away," she snapped. "We'll call you when we need more champagne." But when she turned back to Tamsin, her voice was kind. "A marriage of convenience? For money? Were things that bad?"

"Yes. No." She rubbed her temples. "Sheldon was neglecting Nicole. As Marcos's wife, I can get custody. I can give my sister a home, give her the life she deserves. But I never expected…"

"To fall in love?"

Tamsin nodded miserably.

"Don't be sad. It's a good thing!" Bianca exclaimed.

"You love him, he loves you, and you'll both be happy for the rest of your lives. What's wrong with that?"

"Nothing, if he loved me. But he doesn't. And he won't. He's got his own plans that have nothing to do with me."

"Are you sure?" Daisy asked.

She remembered Marcos's face when he'd said, *There can be no future relationship between us.* The way he pushed her away whenever she got too close. The way he'd so cavalierly canceled their break on the Costa Blanca without explanation the day before. And, worst of all, the dead, hard look in his eyes when he'd said, *I'm not giving up my revenge for you or anyone.*

"I'm sure," she said quietly.

"Don't be silly." Bianca patted her shoulder. "Of course it will work out. Just give him time. No one could help but love you, Tamsin. Once you're married, he'll forget about those other plans and fall for you like a ton of bricks. You'll see. It'll all work out wonderfully."

Tamsin wiped her eyes with the edge of her veil, wanting nothing more than to believe her. "Do you think so?"

"You're wrong, Bianca." Daisy's tense face turned to Tamsin. "If you love him and he doesn't love you, marrying him would be a disaster. It'll kill you. You can't go through with this, Tamsin. You can't." She pulled off Tamsin's veil and leaned forward urgently. "Run away. Trust me. Run as fast as you can."

Tamsin thought of Daisy's words when she was back at Marcos's flat, after she'd dropped her friends at the airport. She stared down at the dream wedding dress that she'd taken home with her in spite of all of Daisy's warnings. She ran her hand softly along the tulle and draped edges of gathered silk. She thought she'd cast aside her girlish romantic dreams long ago, but now she wanted so badly for them to come true she could barely breathe.

Whose view of life did she believe? Bianca's? Or Daisy's?

In the past, she would have said Daisy, hands down.

But that was before. Before she refound her long-lost illusions. Before she'd fallen head over heels in love.

Should she marry Marcos?

Tamsin looked down at the wedding dress spread across Marcos's bed. A moment later she was wearing it again, walking barefoot up and down the hallway. She put on the veil and looked at herself in the mirror. She closed her eyes, imagining that she was walking down the aisle. Marcos was standing at the altar, and his eyes were bright and alive with love...

"*¡Dios mío!*" she heard him say hoarsely.

Whirling around, she saw Marcos standing in the doorway.

Her cheeks went hot. "Stop!" She held up her hand. "Wait!" She tried to run for the hall, out of his sight. "You're not supposed to see me before our wedding day. It's bad luck—"

His laptop bag dropped to the floor with a loud bang as he raced towards her. The door was barely closed behind him before he caught her. He kissed her face through the veil, then pulled back the translucent fabric.

"Tamsin, you're driving me crazy," he whispered against her cheek. "Do you have any idea how much

I've missed you? And to come back here and see you like this—"

He kissed her again savagely, bruising her lips with the force of his desire. She wrapped her arms around him as he picked her up in his arms. As he carried her into the bedroom, her train dragged on the floor behind him, and layers of her tulle skirt floated around her as she pressed her face against his chest.

Her heart started to pound from more than desire. She wanted to tell him.

He carried her to the bed and set her down on the high mattress. He pulled off his coat and then his tie, looking down at her with dark smoldering eyes—and all she could think was that she loved him.

Unbuttoning his cuffs, he removed his shirt, revealing his tanned muscular chest with the trail of black hair that descended beneath his tailored pants—and all she could think was that she loved him.

He pulled off the rest of his clothes, standing in front of her naked, and put one knee on the bed, reaching for her—and all she could think was that she loved him.

He pushed up her voluminous tulle skirts, lowering himself beneath them. She couldn't see him over her skirts, but she could feel his breath, his lips, his mouth tracing the inside of her naked thighs. He slowly stretched her wide and took a long, languorous taste of her, making her back arch and her breasts strain against the tight corset boning of her silk bodice.

She wanted him, but more: she was trembling from the effort of not speaking the words. But she couldn't say them. It would destroy everything between them. He didn't love her back, and he never would.

But that was a blessing. Wasn't it? If he loved her, and couldn't change his vindictive nature, a life with him would not only destroy her, but their children. She couldn't recreate her own horrible childhood for another generation.

I don't love him, she tried to tell herself. *It's just infatuation. Meaningless. Not love...*

His large hands caressed her thighs as he moved up her body. He kissed her neck, running his hands through her hair. She could feel him between her legs, demanding entrance, and her legs spread of their own accord.

"A condom," she gasped at the last minute.

He shook his head, cursing himself under his breath as he reached into the end table. "Forgive me," he said in a low voice. "I lose my reason when I'm with you."

He had the same effect on her. She watched his face, loving every detail. His Roman nose, his high cheek-bones, even the tiny lines between his eyebrows. He was making love to her in her wedding dress. She swallowed, feeling as if her body was going to explode from wanting him and her heart was going to stop beating if she didn't tell him she loved him.

Marcos had missed her.

He wanted to tell her, but the words caught in his throat. He'd gone to Agadir to try to get evidence against Aziz. After today, he would have it. Sheldon was flying to Madrid right now. But that wasn't why Marcos had rushed back from Agadir after one sleepless night in which he'd neither eaten nor slept.

He'd been consumed with thoughts of Tamsin.

Now, as he held her in his arms, he felt an overwhelming sense of relief. As if he'd nearly lost his most prized possession, his fortune, or his dearest friend.

He looked down at her. Her flame-red hair was spread across his pillow, twisted back with diamonds and a gauzy veil. Seeing her in the wedding dress, with her full breasts thrust upwards in the corset and her waist tiny enough to span with his hands, had been a shock to his system. Seeing her now, stretched across his enormous bed, her eyes smoldering up at him with an intoxicating mix of lust and innocence and mystery, was enough to make him lose all pretense of being a civilized man. His whole body was raging with the primitive need to possess her, own her, mark her as his.

She looked up at him, her blue eyes as dark as a summer storm.

"I…you…" She paused, then bit her lip. "You're mussing up my wedding dress."

He ran his hands down her bodice, impatient to feel her breasts, her belly, her smooth skin beneath. "It's in my way."

"The zipper is—"

Before she could even finish the sentence, he'd torn the front of the dress in half, leaving the silk in shreds. He took her breasts in his hands. She gasped in indignation, then pleasure.

"I'll buy you a new dress," he said hoarsely as he kissed down her neck. God, he'd missed her so much, had missed touching her, had missed hearing her voice. How was it possible that, after just one night without her, he'd felt like a man dying of thirst in the desert? "A dozen new dresses, as many as you want."

"A dozen?" She gave a strained laugh, a sexy sound

from low in her throat. "How many times do you intend to marry me?"

He looked down at her, naked beneath him.

"Just once," he told her seriously, but realized to his shock that he no longer had thoughts of divorce.

He had no intention of letting her go. Ever.

He wanted to keep her with him always.

He tried to push the thought out of his mind. He couldn't allow himself to need her. It wasn't good for a man to need anyone. At any moment, she might leave him. She might return to London. She might fall in love with another man.

She might skid her car one rainy night and die.

And he'd be crushed. Helpless. Just like before.

No. He wouldn't let himself think of it.

Closing his eyes, he sheathed himself and thrust himself inside her, filling her completely. She cried out with pleasure. He held himself still, savoring the moment. Holding her like this, his whole being felt illuminated with joy. He felt drunk. Intoxicated. She made him forget everything but how much he needed her...

His eyes flew open. She was becoming too important to him. Too necessary to his happiness in every way. He had to end this. He had to let her go, no matter what it cost him. He had to set her free before something horrible happened, like...

"I love you," she whispered.

He drew back from her with an intake of breath. She was looking at him with her heart shining in her eyes.

"No," he said harshly. "Not in private. Save the sentimental rubbish for when reporters can hear us."

Her face froze. "But I mean it, Marcos. Somehow it's become true. I love you—"

"Stop saying that!" He pulled away from her entirely, grabbing her by the arms and forcing her up in bed. "It's not me you love. It's *this*."

He put his hand between her legs, making her gasp as he fingered her, stroking her tight nub in quick, feather-like movements until she was writhing beneath his touch.

"Please," she panted. "Please listen—"

Ignoring her, he yanked her hands over her head, holding tightly on to her wrists, pushing her back against the headboard. He spread her legs before he thrust into her. Leaning forward, he bit one nipple, sucking hard. She twisted her head from side to side, moaning and bucking her hips. He only slammed into her harder with every thrust.

She gasped out, "Marcos, I lo—"

He covered her mouth with his own before she could finish. He rode her harder and harder, almost hoping that he would hurt her, that she would realize what a beast he was and change her mind and they could go back to how it had been before.

Instead, he felt her shake and quiver and gasp in his arms. Her hips met his with every thrust and, as she came, he couldn't stop her from crying out, "I love you!"

She loved him.

Just the thought shocked him to his core. He didn't want to hurt her. Not Tamsin. She was the first person in twenty years to make him laugh, to make him feel joy, to remind him of the good in the world. He'd die before he hurt her. He wanted to keep her safe always.

Even if it meant saving her from a man like him.

Without finishing, he abruptly pulled away from her. He went to the door and grabbed his robe, which he carelessly tossed at her.

"Get dressed," he said tersely. "You're going."

She blinked at him, struggling to sit up in the tattered remnants of the destroyed wedding dress. "Going?" she repeated in a daze. "Going where?"

"London." He rapidly pulled on his clothes. He couldn't let himself touch her ever again. For her own good, he had to forget about her. Forget the soft touch of her skin, the joy in her laugh, the glow in her eyes. Forget he had ever known her.

"London?" The tormented expression on her face nearly killed him.

He steeled his heart. "To join your sister. The wedding's off."

CHAPTER SEVEN

TAMSIN felt sick.

She watched Marcos reach into his wardrobe and pull a crisply tailored shirt over his muscled torso. Why hadn't she just kept quiet about loving him? Three minutes ago, he'd been ravishing her in her wedding dress, making her scream with pleasure. Now he wouldn't even look at her. Fastest end to a marriage in history, she thought dully.

But she'd known it would happen if she told him she loved him. She'd said it in a foolish hope that he might return her feelings and somehow change for her, forgetting his vindictive plans.

And also because, well, she just hadn't been able to keep herself from blurting it out. She'd never been in love before. But she was already learning how much love could hurt.

Morosely, she looked around the elegant spartan bedroom. Looked at the white goosedown comforter tossed back against the large black lacquer bedframe. The fireplace was also black. Everything in his room was black and white. No room for color. No room for gray.

"You're canceling our wedding because of what I said?"

He finally looked at her as he buttoned up his shirt. "Yes."

Her throat hurt. "But we have to get married. My sister—"

"I have a meeting with your brother this afternoon. I will get you custody of Nicole. I gave you my word."

"My brother is coming here?"

"Sheikh Mohamed al-Maghrib came to see me at my office yesterday, demanding proof of my claims against Aziz. I went to Morocco to get it but, after twenty years, evidence is scant. I need your brother's signed confession."

She asked quietly, "Are you ever going to tell me what they did to you?"

He shook his head. "I'll have my secretary book you on the first flight to London today. My lawyers will be in touch regarding finalization of your sister's custody. It's the easiest end for both of us. We'll never have to see each other again."

Never see him again? *Never?*

Instantly, her heart felt as shredded as her wedding dress. She tried to tell herself it was all for the best but, as she rose to her feet, covering herself with the edges of the torn silk, it was all she could do to keep herself from crying.

"I don't understand why you're making such a big deal over this. Even if it's true that I love you, why should you send me away? Why would you care?"

His expression became hard, almost savage. "Because I care about you, Tamsin," he ground out.

"There—are you satisfied? I care. Enough that I don't want to see you hurt. And if you stay with me, you will be."

It was true. She knew that he would hurt her and if they had children, they would be hurt as well. She should be grateful for his mercy in letting her go. She should run as fast as she could and never look back.

But she couldn't run. She couldn't even move.

She loved him.

"The Sheikh thinks I've insulted his family," Marcos said grimly, "and, unless I can prove otherwise within two days, it will mean war. I want you a million miles away, but London will have to do."

"You're trying to protect me from them?"

He shook his head. "Not just them. Anyone who loves me ends up hurt or worse. I won't let that happen. Not to you." He turned away, then paused to give her one last look from the door. "Goodbye, Tamsin."

He turned back towards the door and she realized he intended to walk away from her for ever.

"What if I'm pregnant?"

He paused and, without turning around, he spoke in a low voice. "I will always take care of you both. You'll have all the money you will ever need. But you'll both be better off without me."

She put her hands to her cheeks. How could she argue with him when everything he said was true? But, as he started to walk away, she couldn't let him go.

She ran towards him, blocking him from the door. "I'm staying with you."

He gave an angry, exasperated sigh. "Tamsin—"

"Just for your meeting with my brother. I don't care

what you say. My first priority is Nicole's welfare. For all I know, when you see Sheldon you'll forget all about helping me and just push him out of a window or something. I can't allow Nicole to be left in Camilla's custody."

"'Push him out of a window?" He looked incredulous. "I have a little more self-control than that."

"I'm not leaving until I know my sister's safe."

His eyes were as cold and gray as an arctic winter. "She's safe for now. Sheldon and his wife took her to London last night and left her with an old nanny, Allison something."

"Allison Holland?"

"Yes."

She breathed a sigh of relief. If Nicole was with Allison, that meant she was warm and fed and properly looked after. She'd once been Tamsin's nanny too.

"He's trying to appear like a responsible guardian," Marcos continued grimly. "He must know we're going to seek custody."

"All the more reason for me to stay and help sort things out."

"You're wasting your time. A few hours isn't going to change my mind about us."

"Fine, I get it. No wedding. Getting married to you wasn't exactly my idea, anyway." Resolutely, she pushed away the heartache and all the glowing hopes she'd wrapped in the beautiful dress that was now tattered around her shoulders. Ending their relationship was for the best, she repeated to herself firmly. "I'm staying for Nicole. It has nothing to do with you."

His jaw twitched. "Fine."

"Fine."

He turned to go.

"Marcos?"

"What?"

"I want to thank you." Taking a deep breath, she forced herself to meet his eyes. She forced herself to speak the truth she knew in her heart, even though it hurt her. "Thank you for not loving me."

Tamsin sat in Marcos's modern office in the heart of the financial district. The broad windows behind his desk showed much of the length of the Paseo de Castellana. She could almost see Marcos's penthouse some distance away. She wished she was back there, in his arms, in the comfort and pleasure of his bedroom, before she'd ever realized she loved him.

Gripping the edges of her chair, she blew on her tea for the tenth time. She felt Marcos's hands on her shoulders as he stood behind her, but it made her more nervous than ever.

"Your brother cannot hurt you any more."

"He can keep Nicole from having a decent childhood."

"It's not going to happen."

Her hands were shaking. She took her first sip of tea, only to discover that it was quite cold. No wonder. Marcos's secretary had brought it to her when they'd arrived, and for the last twenty minutes she'd been breathing on it like a pregnant woman at Lamaze practice.

At the thought, Tamsin's hand involuntarily went to her belly. She forced herself to be calm. She wasn't pregnant and soon she would have the proof. She would leave Marcos as he wished, leaving his darkness and revenge far behind her, and start a fresh new life with Nicole. The life Nicole deserved.

She should have been grateful.

Instead, leaving Marcos felt like going to prison for life.

"What did you mean earlier?" Marcos asked abruptly.

"When?" she asked, although she already knew.

His hands were still on her shoulders as he looked down at her, his face an inscrutable mask. "When you thanked me for not loving you."

Tamsin immediately felt her fingers and toes turn to ice. But he'd asked her the question. He deserved an answer.

"Because of your need for revenge," she said quietly. "I can't live with a man whose whole life is tangled up in rage. Marrying you would poison me. It would poison our children. But, even knowing this, I still wouldn't have been able to resist you." Their eyes locked. "Thank you for not loving me."

His hands tightened. "Tamsin—"

"The Winters are here, *señor*," one of his assistants interrupted over the intercom.

Marcos pressed a button on his desk. "Send them in." Releasing the button, he clenched his jaw. "I'm surprised that Winter would bring his wife."

"I'm not." She took another sip. Still shaken from telling Marcos the truth, and now facing Camilla into the bargain, she needed all the fortification she could get. "She has always been the Lady Macbeth type, pushing him into everything. Before they were married, he wasn't nearly so bad."

The door opened and Tamsin rose shakily to her feet.

"Señor y Señora Winter," the secretary announced. Then, in accented English, "Can I get you some tea? Coffee?"

"Nothing," Camilla said.

"I'd like a Scotch," Sheldon said.

"I'll get it," Marcos said, staring fiercely at Sheldon. The secretary left with a nod.

Her half-brother squirmed uncomfortably under his gaze. Looking at Marcos's razor-sharp jaw and clenched fists, Tamsin wondered if he could really throw Sheldon out the window. He looked as if he were holding on to his icy veneer only by the barest self-control and, at any moment, he might take her brother's throat in his hands and wring his life away.

Marcos turned on his heel and poured a small glass of Scotch. He presented it to Sheldon with a smile that was nothing more than a flash of sharp white teeth. "Have a seat."

"Not until you tell me why you've summoned us here," Sheldon said. "You've got some nerve to—"

"Oh, do sit down, Sheldon," Camilla snapped. She perched on a seat with her skinny legs tucked beneath her and her expensive handbag on her lap. "Let Mr. Ramirez speak. The sooner we're done here, the sooner I can return to that dear, dear child."

"Dear child?" Tamsin gasped. "You starved and exploited her so you could spend her trust fund on plastic surgery and ski trips!"

Camilla gave her a pointed smile. "I was merely giving the child a chance to experience her first taste of independence. Because of you, really."

"Me?"

"Of course. You had such a cloistered upbringing, and yet you turned out to be the biggest slut in London. A change of child-rearing technique seemed to be in order."

"Oh, you—" Jumping out of her chair, Tamsin longed to slap Camilla's tight, smug face. But Marcos stopped her.

"I suggest," he said tersely to Sheldon, "that you put a rein on that cat. Before you both regret it."

Sheldon looked startled, as if having any control over Camilla was an idea that had never occurred to him before.

"How dare you?" Camilla's nose quivered in outrage. It was, Tamsin supposed, the only part of her face that hadn't been artificially stretched or frozen into immobility. "You are the one who will regret speaking that way to me. The price of Nicole's custody papers just increased by a hundred thousand pounds."

"You are *selling* my sister?" Tamsin cried.

"Why shouldn't I? Her trust fund is almost gone. The chit is worthless to us. I could sell her for far more elsewhere. How much do you suppose a little blonde girl is worth to a man like Aziz?"

For a moment, Tamsin couldn't breathe. "Don't you have a soul?"

"Of course I do." Camilla looked pleased with herself. "And the courts will believe it. If you try to take her, I will convince them I love that child as my very own. I'll smear you both in the press with every loathsome secret you have. Even if I have to make everything up."

Tamsin glanced at Marcos, who'd been listening silently from the swivel chair behind his desk. Why was he doing nothing, saying nothing?

Camilla glanced down at her long, perfectly manicured fingernails. "Better for you to pay. I know Mr. Ramirez can certainly afford it. Nicole's price was two million pounds, but now it's a hundred thousand more. And the more of my time you take, the more I will charge. It's only fair."

Marcos folded his hands behind his neck, tilting his head as if in thought. "And you agree with your wife, Mr. Winter?"

Sheldon bit his lip. "Well, of course I wouldn't actually sell Nicole to some harem somewhere. That would be quite barbaric—"

"Shut up, Sheldon," his wife hissed. Looking abashed, he fell silent and took a furtive sip of Scotch.

"I see." Slowly, Marcos stood up. "I have another deal for you," he said pleasantly.

"A better one?" Camilla demanded.

"Yes, I think so."

"Go ahead," she said airily.

"You might have been able to bully Tamsin, but your methods will not work with me. I am not a naïve twenty-three-year-old with a kind heart. I am," he said with a smile that sent a chill through Tamsin's body, "a monster like you. And worse. I will give you two options. First— you both go to jail for child neglect. I already have evidence that will convince any court, as well as the financial ability to secure a verdict if that proves necessary. The scandal will be the final blow to your business. No woman will buy cosmetics from a company that's linked to child abuse. You won't even have enough money left to hire a decent lawyer, so I expect you'll go for the maximum sentence." Standing in front of her, he leaned back against his desk. "That is my best offer."

"I don't have to listen to this," Camilla said. "Sheldon, we're leaving—"

She started to stand up, but Marcos signaled for her to sit back into her chair.

For the first time that Tamsin had ever seen, Camilla was speechless.

"My second option," Marcos continued as if nothing had happened, "is not nearly so generous. You know how I kidnapped Tamsin. That was nothing. I can make you both disappear. No one will even know what happened to you. You will just be another set of bones beneath the sand for archeologists to find in a hundred years."

Camilla bit her lip, clutching her Prada handbag to her scrawny chest.

"I say," Sheldon protested feebly, "you're scaring my wife—"

"You are the one who should be scared, Winter." Marcos turned on him. "I've spent twenty years dreaming of the day I would make you pay."

Sheldon looked astonished. "Me? I know you have some grudge against Aziz, but what do you have against me? To the best of my knowledge, we've never even met."

"Twenty years ago, you bought a formula for an anti-aging cream that Aziz stole from my father. Your lawyers got a crooked judge to award you the patent. My father was ruined, then died with my mother and brother. All these years, I've dreamed of taking revenge. And now that day has finally come."

Tamsin gaped at him. Marcos's father had created the formula for the original anti-aging cream? She knew the product well. It had been developed into W.I.'s best-selling line. She herself had often used the ConcealStick to hide dark circles after a sleepless night. And, for all these years, Sheldon had taken credit for the formula. It had been his one success at the company, the one thing that their father had ever praised him for.

He'd stolen it from Marcos's father.

And Marcos's whole family had died, including the young brother he'd loved so much. But how? How had it happened? And how had he survived the pain?

Marcos stood before him, taut as a cocked rifle, his hands balled into fists. Tamsin wanted to take him in her arms, to tell him everything would be all right, to offer the comfort of her body and the comfort of her love.

Then she remembered that he had no interest in her comfort. To the contrary. He looked as if he really might rip out Sheldon's heart with his bare hands.

It frightened her.

Her half-brother's red face was beaded with sweat. "I'd already had three failures in R&D. My father was ready to kill me. I saw the formula and had to take it. But I didn't mean to hurt anyone! I swear to God, if I'd known someone would die, I'd never have…"

"Right. You just took the formula and lived off the profits for the last twenty years. But now Winter International has fallen apart. What you didn't do to ruin the company, I did."

"You intentionally ruined me?" Sheldon blurted out.

"Yes. And I'll do more. You deserve to suffer, as my family did."

Hands clenched, Marcos took a step towards him.

And Tamsin suddenly forgot her own fear in the terror that he might kill her brother. Whatever Marcos was, he wasn't a murderer. She wouldn't let him become one in a moment of duress.

Leaping to her feet, she grabbed his shoulder. He whirled to face her, his dark eyes wild, and for a moment she actually thought he might hit her.

"Marcos," she said softly.

He recognized her, and some of the anger faded.

He took a deep breath and turned back to Sheldon. "Here's what you're going to do. You're going to give custody of your sister to Tamsin. And you're going to give me a signed confession about the formula that I can use as proof of Aziz al-Maghrib's original theft. Do both these things and I will let you live. You will be penniless, and you will likely go to jail, but I will let you live."

Sheldon licked his blubbery lips. "Yes," he said with a resigned sigh. He rubbed his balding head wearily. "Yes. Justice would almost be a relief after all these years." He turned to Tamsin. "Take Nicole. Just take her. God knows I haven't been a fit guardian."

"Coward!" Camilla thundered, standing up straight and glaring at Sheldon. "I always knew you were weak. I wash my hands of you." She pulled her handbag up on her shoulder. "Our marriage is over. I'm going to be with a real man who won't cower and cave in and talk about *justice*."

She stormed out. Sheldon watched her go with red-rimmed eyes, but didn't try to stop her. He looked up at Marcos. "Now, what do you want me to sign?"

* * *

So this was what revenge felt like.

Marcos held the confession in his hand, staring at it while he waited for Tamsin to return from walking her brother to the elevator. He slowly set the paper down on his desk next to the signed custody agreement. He pushed both papers around, looking at Sheldon's signature. After twenty years, he'd finally crushed Sheldon Winter. He'd finally gotten proof of Aziz al-Maghrib's crime. He'd won.

But he'd thought it would feel…different. Where was his triumph? Where was his sense of peace?

Thank you for not loving me.

Abruptly, he turned his swivel chair to face the wide wall of windows. The sky was bright blue with an unrelenting sun, appropriate for a hot September day, but shadows were all around, cast by the tall skyscrapers of the Azca district. He looked down at the Castellana. Ten stories below, people were sitting outside at the sidewalk cafés, enjoying the warmth of the sun.

He had a sudden memory of his family's vacation in southern England when, after three days of rain, the clouds had abruptly cleared and they'd run out on to the beach to feel the heat of the sun. Even now, he could close his eyes and hear the distant echo of his brother's laughter, feel his mother's arms around his shoulders, recall the comforting sound of his father's voice calling over the roar of the ocean.

But, almost instantly, the memories were buried beneath the loud squeal of tires and sickening crunch of metal that he'd imagined so many times.

Marcos's hands tightened into fists.

His father had made the mistake of showing an early

version of his anti-aging formula to Aziz al-Maghrib, the scion of the wealthy family that controlled the largest harvest of argan oil in the world. He'd hoped to convince Aziz to make an investment. The man had decided to make a quick million by selling the formula to Sheldon instead.

And while they'd been on vacation, after their one bright, sunny day, his parents had found out that W.I.'s team of unethical lawyers had managed to convince the courts the giant cosmetics company had created the anti-aging cream. After years of development, the small pharmaceutical firm owned by Marcos's father had lost everything.

They had even lost their lives.

He sat forward, pressing his knuckles against his eyes. If revenge didn't work, then what? What was left?

It would work, he told himself fiercely. It had to. He just hadn't finished the job. He'd ruined Sheldon Winter, and he would make sure the man went to jail. Then he would see Aziz humiliated, disinherited and utterly shamed in front of his whole tribe.

If that still didn't work, he would think of something. He would taunt Aziz into a fight. He wanted to destroy him. Only that could finally bury the nightmares that haunted him.

Marrying you would poison me. It would poison our children. But knowing this, I still wouldn't have been able to resist you. Thank you for not loving me.

He closed his eyes, taking a deep breath. Tamsin was right. Marrying him would have destroyed her. Pushing her away was the only truly selfless thing he'd ever done in his whole life.

He looked up as she came through the office door. She was wearing a simple blue dress, modest but chic, hiding her curves but somehow accentuating all the right places. The indigo silk matched her eyes, made them deep as the ocean against her pale skin and fiery red hair.

She'd been an oasis, he thought. A drink of clear water in the dry desert of his life.

She sat in the nearest chair, crossing her legs. "I talked to Sheldon," she said. "He's honestly sorry. He says he intended to pay back our trust funds when he could, and I know I shouldn't but I do believe him."

His eyes involuntarily traced the shape of her legs—shapely calves and sleek ankles that ended in high-heeled black leather shoes. "He slapped you. He tried to force you into a marriage you didn't want. Is he sorry for that too?"

"Part of that was Camilla. She was screaming at him that he'd do it if he were any sort of a man. She also assured him that Nicole would be perfectly fine on her own for a week or two and, seeing as she's a woman and supposed to be intuitive at child-rearing, he figured she'd know." She held up her hand. "Don't get me wrong. It's not like I think he's a great guy or anything, but after a while…I might be able to forgive him."

"I won't. There's no excuse for hitting a woman. Ever."

"Maybe. But I'm not going to waste another second of my life being angry at him. I'm starting my life fresh and new. For myself. For my sister." Coming around to his side of the desk, she wrapped her arms around his neck. "You did this. You saved us." She kissed his cheek. "Thank you."

He wanted her so badly, it was intolerable. Not just her body. He wanted her optimism, her cheerfulness, her peace.

He wanted what a life with her would have offered, if things were different.

It would be so easy to love her…

He pushed her away, not wanting to feel her touch, not wanting to be tempted by all the feelings that rushed through him when she was near. "It was nothing."

She sat down in the chair. "So it's over."

"No," he said. "It's not even close to over."

She looked at him, her sea-blue eyes tinged with alarm. "Please don't do more to Sheldon. Not just for his sake, but mine. He's giving up Winter International. He only took the job as CEO because my father insisted, and he didn't want to be the one who made it go bankrupt after sixty years of business. Isn't that funny? He didn't want it. I did, but my father said that it was a man's world and I should stay out of it."

Marcos shook his head in disbelief. "Your father was a fool."

"He was almost sixty when I was born. I don't think he ever understood people. He only knew how to boss and bully and hit. He was the most vindictive, angry man I've ever known." She started to say more, then stopped herself. Marcos guessed what she'd been about to say: *until I met you*.

She cleared her throat. "Anyway, it never occurred to me that Sheldon might feel trapped too. He's going to go back home and open a golfing shop. He's always loved golf. And I had this crazy idea." She lowered her eyes shyly, giving him a dimpled smile. "Maybe I could try and lead Winter International myself. What do you think?"

Though she tried to sound casual, he could hear the tremor beneath her question. He pushed it aside.

"Your brother is not going to open a golfing shop," Marcos said. "He's going to jail."

"Marcos, please." Tamsin stood up, twisting her hands together. "Let it go."

There was no point in arguing with her. Marcos turned away in his swivel chair to face the windows. Sunlight hit his face. Warmly. Lovingly. Reproachfully.

He turned back to face her. "You have the papers that will give you custody. Go to London. I will tell my lawyers to expect your call. Your sister needs you."

She took a deep breath. "I don't want to leave you like this."

"That was our agreement," he said, keeping his face expressionless. "We both know it's for the best."

"Yes. I know." She stepped towards him and, in the sunlight, her hair was as red as roses. Her eyes glowed the truest blue he'd ever seen, like Christmas lights, or sapphires, or the warm summer sky. She placed her slender white hand on his shoulder. "But I don't want to leave you. Please, Marcos. Give up your revenge." She whispered, "Choose me instead."

He shook his head, pulling away from her with a bitter laugh. "If you think that after twenty years I can just let Aziz get away with what he did, then you don't know me at all. In spite of your claim to love me."

She knelt before him pleadingly, resting her hands

on his knee. "My father let himself be consumed by the need for revenge, and it ripped my family apart. No matter what you think it will do for you, it won't. It will only feed the darkness in your soul and make you want more. Give it up. Please." Her eyes filled with tears. "I do love you. I do. That's why I'm asking you to let Sheldon and Aziz go."

Hearing her say she loved him did strange things to his insides. It made him feel dizzy, as if the earth were shaking beneath his feet. It made him feel uncertain of his understanding of the world and his place in it.

He didn't like it. And yet…

The pull she had over him was magnetic. He came closer to her, watching the rise and fall of her breathing. Looking down at her, he gently stroked her cheek, her throat, the bare skin of her collar-bone.

He had to send her away. For her own good. As soon as possible.

But he didn't want to do it. He wanted to make love to her. On his desk, at home, everywhere. He wanted her to wear his wedding ring. He wanted to brand her as irrevocably his. To show every other man on earth that she belonged to him and him alone.

He wanted her to be his wife.

He wanted her to bear his child.

He wanted to wake up to her face every morning for the rest of his life.

And that was when he felt the horrifying truth like a bullet to his heart: he was already in love with her.

CHAPTER EIGHT

BREATHLESS, Tamsin waited for his answer.

He stared at her for several moments. There was a strange light in his eyes. What was he thinking? Was it possible he'd give up his revenge? Could they be happy after all?

Then he spoke. His voice was weary, tired, a hundred years old.

"Tamsin, I can't let Aziz go free. He must be punished. It's the only way I'll ever find peace."

She exhaled as hope left her.

"I'm sorry. I know it's not what you wanted. But it's the only answer I can give." He reached down to caress her cheek. "I can't lie to you. Not to you."

Stumbling backward, she flinched from his hand, afraid that if he touched her, if he kissed her, she would fall into his arms and never have the strength to pull away again.

So quickly that she might have imagined it, his handsome face contorted in an expression of hurt. He abruptly dropped his hand.

"I will arrange for your return to London." He

pressed the intercom on his desk. "Amelita, please book the next flight for—"

"No." She ripped his hand away from the button. "I can't just let you throw your life away! I won't!"

"*¿Señor?*" His executive secretary's voice spoke through the intercom. "*¿Puedo ayudarle?*"

"*Un momento*, Amelita." Releasing the button, he looked at Tamsin steadily. "You can't stop me from getting justice for my family."

"It's not justice. It's revenge and it won't make you happy. It won't bring you peace." She tightened her grip on his hand. "It's how my father lost his friends, his marriages, the love of his children. He was always angry, always determined to take an eye for an eye. But he wasn't always like that, I heard. His first wife had an affair with his best friend. It broke his heart and he didn't stop until he crushed them both. But, even when they were penniless outcasts, he wasn't happy. He was always watching and waiting for the next person to betray him. Sometimes he would take the first hit, to beat them to the punch."

Marcos clenched his hands into fists. "I'm not like that."

"Maybe not yet. But you will be." She glanced at the papers on his desk. "You've got Sheldon's confession. Did it make you feel a sense of peace?"

He clenched his jaw. "It's a start."

"It's a lie. Revenge won't make you feel better, and it won't bring your family back."

He jerked his hand away. "You know nothing of my family."

"So tell me!" she nearly shouted. "Tell me what happened!"

He stood up from his chair and, without looking at her, crossed to the wet bar. "Sheldon and Aziz ruined my family and caused their deaths. Isn't that enough?"

She rose unsteadily to her feet. "How? How did they do it?"

He poured himself a short bourbon. "I don't want to talk about it."

"Yes, you do," she said. "I think you're tired of not talking about it. I think not talking about it is killing you."

Holding the glass, he gave a scornful laugh. "That doesn't even make sense."

"They ruined your father's business, I get that. But how did that cause their deaths?" She folded her arms across her chest. "You've been planning revenge for so long, I would think you'd be eager to explain the details of their crimes."

He came closer to her. With a quick swallow of bourbon, he set his glass down on his desk. When he looked at her, all the mockery was gone from his expression.

"Tamsin, just let me go," he said quietly. "It's better for me to face Aziz than always wonder if he's behind us, waiting to strike. I will take care of him. Then you won't have to worry." He reached for her, softly stroking her hair, and she couldn't move away. "I need that. I need to know you're safe and happy."

Anger pulsed through her. "Don't you *dare* say you're doing this for me! Do you honestly think that ruining Aziz and throwing Sheldon in jail will make you feel better?"

He slammed his open palm against his desk.

"Yes!" he exploded. "*¡Maldito sea!* It must!"

His anger frightened her, but she wouldn't back down. Reaching up to grasp his shoulders, she looked intently into his eyes.

"Just tell me. Tell me how your family died."

He clenched his jaw. "*Madre de Dios*, you never give up."

"Right." *Not when it comes to loving you.* "So you might as well tell me."

"And if I do, you will leave Madrid at once? No more arguments? No more attempts to save my soul?"

She pressed her lips together silently.

"I want your word," he demanded.

No, she thought. *No, no, no.*

"Yes," she whispered.

He sat down heavily in his chair. Looking out through the wide expanse of windows, he rubbed his forehead with his hand. "I was twelve years old. My family was on vacation in England. I knew my father was having some kind of difficulty at work, but we were sure he'd win his case. How could he not? Justice was on our side." He closed his eyes. "But we lost my father's patent, a patent it had taken ten years of research to develop. My father's company, his fortune, his life's work were all wiped away in the blink of an eye."

"And that was my brother's fault." Her cheeks burned with shame. Standing behind him, she put her hand on his shoulder. "I'm so sorry."

He continued talking, staring out through the window as if he hadn't heard her. "Overnight, my father turned from a giant to a walking shadow. My mother couldn't stop weeping. My brother Diego was only nine, and he didn't understand. Neither did I. But I was the oldest son. They'd hurt my family. I had to make them pay."

He rubbed his forehead wearily.

"So what did you do?" she asked softly.

"I ran away." He glanced back at her with an ironic, self-mocking smile. "I'd been saving money to buy Diego a new kite for his birthday, and so I thought I had enough to fly back to Madrid. I was going to find the men who'd hurt us and force them to give everything back."

So young, she thought. He really had been on a quest for revenge for twenty years. Two-thirds of his life. What would that do to someone?

"I hitchhiked to Heathrow Airport," he said. "My parents guessed where I was going and followed me in the rental car. It was a rainy night, very dark, and they skidded around a slippery bend on the M25. They crashed into a slow-moving truck and were crushed beneath the wheels. My parents died instantly. My brother lived for an hour. At least, that's what I was told. I wasn't there when they died. I was at the airport, trying to buy a flight to Madrid for twelve pounds."

"Oh, Marcos," she whispered as she took his hands in her own. Tears spilled over her lashes.

His jaw line was dark with five o'clock shadow and his handsome face was haggard as he looked at her. The expression in his tortured eyes cut through her.

"You blame me for their deaths," he said hoarsely.

"No!" Desperately, she kissed his hand, pressing it against her cheek. "It wasn't your fault, Marcos. *It wasn't*. You were just a boy. You had no way to know that—"

"Stop lying!" Pulling away from her, he rose unsteadily to his feet. "You blame me. I can see it in your eyes."

"I don't blame you." She brought her hands to her mouth with a sudden intake of breath. "Oh, my God. No wonder you're so angry," she said softly. "For twenty years you've been dreaming of revenge against my brother and Aziz. But it's not true. That's not what you want. The one you really want to punish is yourself."

For a moment he seemed to sway towards her, then his face hardened. "So stop trying to save me. Leave me in peace to do what I must do."

"Marcos, please. It wasn't your fault. You have to know that. I love you—"

"Take back your love, Tamsin," he said harshly. "I don't deserve it. I don't want it."

"Marcos!" She tried to reach for him, but he wouldn't let her. He opened the office door and looked back at her with strange dead eyes.

"No more delays. No more excuses. I expect you to honor your promise now." He turned to speak to his assistant. "Amelita, Miss Winter will be leaving Madrid at once. Please arrange her flight."

"*Sí, señor.*"

He faced Tamsin. "In the future, if there is anything you ever need, money or help of any sort—or if there's a child—you will contact my lawyers immediately. Promise me."

"Don't leave—"

"*Promise*," he demanded savagely.

"I promise." Tears were streaming down her cheeks. "Please, Marcos. Stay. Talk to me. There must be another way…"

"There is nothing to discuss. Your future is in London, and my path lies in Morocco." Blinking fast, he turned away. "Goodbye, Tamsin."

The home of Sheikh Mohamed ibn Battuta al-Maghrib was an imposing three-story citadel with crenellated towers situated on the Tata River. Surrounded by a *ksar*, or fortified village, the kasbah was set to the far east of Agadir in a desert oasis near the Anti-Atlas Mountains.

Narrowing her eyes to see through the decorative *mashrabiyya* screen on the window, Tamsin watched the sun set over the mountains, the rosy light moving over vivid ochre- and violet-colored rock. She folded her hands together to keep them from shaking. After everything that had happened today, she should have been numb.

She'd just lost the love of her life.

An hour later, she'd discovered that she wasn't pregnant.

Strange to think she'd been so terrified of having Marcos's child. Now, she mourned the loss of the dream. She imagined their baby gurgling in her arms, smiling and cooing, looking up at her with the dark, serious eyes of his father.

No child meant no hope. No reason to see Marcos again. No living memory of her love for him.

Tamsin knew she was young and unprepared to be a mother. It would have been inconvenient and difficult. But now she knew it would have also been wonderful, and she grieved the loss as if she'd always known she wanted Marcos's child.

What next? Would she lose her family's company too?

"The Sheikh will see you now," his dour aide-de-camp said in heavily accented English.

"Thank you."

The older man pursed his lips disapprovingly. He held the door open for her at a distance, as if afraid to be close to any woman mad enough to travel alone to the isolated village of the al-Maghribs, known throughout Morocco not just for their extensive argan fields but for their production of daggers and guns.

It was indeed a man's world. Sheldon had offered to travel with her, but she had refused. He was busy dealing with lawyers in the dissolution of his marriage. And he'd already helped her more than he knew, by explaining the reason Camilla was so eager to get a divorce.

Tamsin had wanted to come here on her own. To prove she could. To show she was strong enough to succeed in a man's world.

To prove she could keep breathing with a heart shattered into pieces.

She followed the man down the hall and stepped into the reception hall, holding her long robes above the floor. A veil covered her hair, out of respect for the man she was about to see, and she entered with her back straight and her head held high.

She padded across the thickly embroidered carpets. Above her, the soaring ceiling was painted with volutes and interlacing patterns. Elegant furniture filled the room. The Sheikh sat at the center on a silken sofa, smoking a hookah. A low desk was in front of him and a male servant stood behind him silently.

He looked up, but made no effort to rise. "Ah, my

nephew's runaway bride," he said in cultured English, regarding her with bright, inquisitive eyes. "I am curious to know why you would wish to see me. Please sit down."

She took the nearby chair he indicated. On the plane from Madrid she'd practiced phrases meant to charm and cajole, but now she was far too nervous to be anything but blunt. "Thank you. I'll get right to the point."

He nodded.

"My brother has decided to retire from Winter International, so I am taking over the company. I've come to ask you to keep the business deal you had with Sheldon—to sell us this year's harvest of argan oil on credit, interest-free."

"And why should I do that, miss? Have you returned to Morocco to marry my nephew?"

"No."

He shrugged expressively. "The deal included a bride."

"And my family has provided you with one." Heart pounding at her own audacity, she met his eyes. "This morning, my brother's wife, Camilla, left Sheldon to be with your nephew. As I understand from her call to my brother, she has been seeing Aziz secretly for weeks. She filed for divorce just hours ago—with the assistance of your lawyers, I believe. She has told Sheldon she intends to marry Aziz, which I believe you yourself already know."

He blinked, then gave her a slow smile. "You are very quick."

"Thank you."

"Are you sure you won't change your mind and

marry my nephew? You seem far more useful than the bride he has chosen for himself."

She hid a shudder. "I'm afraid that's out of the question."

"I know there are rumors that he killed his first wife, but those are lies. She died in an accident. I saw it. Does that sway you?"

She shook her head. "But I'm glad to know, for Camilla's sake."

He gave her a wry smile. "Do not be too glad for her. My nephew is not a murderer, but he is hardly a paragon. It is a hard life he will give her. I suspect that she is more in love with my wealth than with him and, as she has no social connections and is unlikely to produce an heir, I can only guess that a voracious appetite in...other pursuits drives them together. A most unpromising match, in my view, but—" he shrugged ironically, "—who am I to stand in the way of love? You are correct, young woman. Your family has indeed given my nephew a bride. So I am bound by honor to fulfill my end of the deal."

He snapped his fingers. His servant brought him a ledger and a pen, which he spread across his desk. Less than five minutes later, Tamsin walked out of the kasbah in amazement. She had everything she'd wanted.

Then she looked up.

No, she didn't have everything she wanted. Not even close. Her heart leapt into her throat as she watched Marcos climb out of a dusty truck parked near the *wadi*. He tossed a rucksack over his shoulder and, slamming the door, headed towards the kasbah.

Then he saw her. He stopped so abruptly that his

boots kicked up a cloud of dust, and stared at her as if she were a ghost.

"Tamsin." He licked his lips uncertainly. "What are you doing here?"

"Marcos," she whispered. Her whole body trembled as she took a step towards him. She'd spent all day crying as she'd traveled here, telling herself to forget him, trying to remember every horrible thing he'd ever said or done. Seeing him now sent her reeling. She wanted to take him in her arms, kiss his troubled face and tell him that she loved him. She wanted to beg him again to give up his desire for revenge, to love her instead.

But his face had already hardened. "If you've come to try and stop me from getting justice against Aziz, you've wasted your time. I won't let him live unpunished while my family is dead. He has to pay."

It was the hard, cold slap in the face that she needed. Beg him to love her, just so he could reject her again? No.

"Don't worry." She straightened, pressing her fingernails into her palms to distract herself from the ache in her heart. "I'm not here for you. I came to see the Sheikh about the argan oil."

"Oil?" He blinked at her as if she'd just spoken in Greek. "What are you talking about?"

"The business deal. I told you. I'm trying to save Winter International." She gave him a brittle smile. "So far, so good. The Sheikh agreed to sell me the entire harvest on credit."

He shook his head with a frown. "But how did you get here? I told Amelita—"

"You told her to get me the first flight out of Madrid,

and she did." She held up her hand. "This is just a stopover. I'll barely make it to Agadir before my flight leaves for London. And, for what it's worth, I intend to pay you royalties for your father's formula. As soon as I can get the company stabilized, I will pay you every pound plus interest."

He looked shaken. "But it's not your debt to repay."

"It's my family's obligation, which means it's now mine. If you still have a desire to destroy us, there's nothing I can do. Just as there's nothing I can do to stop you from drowning in your own hatred."

His jaw tightened as he pulled his rucksack higher against his shoulder. "You were willing to throw your life away to save your sister's. What is the difference between that and what I'm now forced to do?"

She shook her head incredulously. "You really don't see the difference?"

"No. We both want to protect the people we love."

"You're not protecting them. You're avenging them. Your family would never have wanted this life for you. They would have wanted you to forgive and have a life of your own. Not to punish yourself as you've done for the last twenty years. The way you've chosen, always looking back, always angry and vindictive—it's a living death, Marcos."

His expression changed. "After what Aziz nearly did to you—what he did to his first wife—don't you think he should suffer?"

"You're the one who deserves to stop suffering," she snapped. "Why can't you see that?"

"Tamsin—"

"And, for what it's worth, Aziz isn't a murderer, just

a thief. The Sheikh told me he didn't murder his wife, he witnessed the accident. So if you intend to punish him for stealing the formula, you might as well come after me too, since it's my company that profited most from the theft."

His face contorted. "I would never hurt you, Tamsin. Never. You could be the mother of my child."

"No." Blinking hard so he wouldn't see her tears, she forced out the words. "I'm not pregnant. I just found out for sure. So that's one thing you don't need to worry about. Don't worry about me either. I'll never trouble you again."

She turned away, heading towards her small rental car, which was parked near the stone houses in the palm grove.

"You're really not pregnant?" he asked. "You're telling me the truth?"

She turned back to face him. His face was half-hidden by shadows in the fading dusk.

"Yes," she said quietly. "It's the truth."

He clenched his jaw, rubbing his forehead. The muscles revealed by his tight T-shirt were hard and strained. She knew every inch of his body so well. Too bad he'd never really let her know his soul. Remembering everything good between them, she felt like crying.

Almost, she thought. She'd almost known him. She'd almost been pregnant. They'd almost had a chance at a life together.

"Goodbye, Marcos." She turned away.

He grabbed her arm. "Tamsin, wait."

She could feel the touch of his hand up and down her

arm, up and down her whole body. She didn't look at him. She was afraid that, if she did, she'd grab hold of him and never let go. "What do you want?"

For a moment, he didn't speak. "I…I don't want to lose you."

Sucking in her breath, she whirled to face him. Was it possible that he had changed his mind? That he'd realized the futility of revenge and wanted to truly experience life—a life filled with forgiveness and joy?

Raking his hand through his hair, he licked his lips. "Look, just stay with me. After I deal with Aziz, we can talk. Find a middle ground. Perhaps you and your sister could come and live in Madrid. Then we could be together. We could…date."

Her heart, which had soared at his first words, fell hard to the ground. He hadn't told her he loved her. He hadn't asked for a commitment. He was still so focused on what had happened twenty years ago that he wasn't even willing to travel to London for her sister's sake. He was still intent on revenge and obviously not willing to change.

And yet he expected her to drag her sister across Europe and give up her family's company to date him in Madrid.

She swallowed. Not trusting herself to speak, she shook her head.

The momentary light in his eyes faded. Shielding his face from the setting sun, he looked away, clenching his jaw. "Then I guess this is goodbye," he said finally. "Enjoy your life, Tamsin."

She swallowed, still fighting the urge to throw herself at his feet, to beg him to love her, to beg him to live. She forced herself to turn from him, whirling away in a flare of long robes before he could see her weep.

"Enjoy your death," she choked out. She nearly ran the rest of the way to the palm grove, then drove down the dusty mountain road as fast as her little car would go. She didn't look back and didn't even let herself burst into sobs until the kasbah of Oukenzate was just a memory behind her.

Marcos watched her go until her car was nothing more than a cloud of dust on the mountain horizon.

It was better this way, he tried to tell himself as he turned towards the kasbah. He was no good for her. No good for anyone. Loving him just ruined people's lives.

But, as he entered the reception hall, his body still hurt as if he'd been pummeled, as if he'd just lost a fight. Stiffly, he greeted the Sheikh with a bow and respectful words in Arabic.

The Sheikh returned his greeting with grave courtesy. "I trust you brought the proof?" he said in English.

"As promised."

"The council of elders will hear your charges. My nephew must be given the chance to defend himself."

Marcos frowned. "You're putting him on trial? I thought my evidence was for you alone."

He tilted his head, examining Marcos closely. "The charges you've made are punishable by death. By our law, my nephew cannot be sentenced without the council's agreement."

Death? Marcos was stunned. "I thought the punishment was exile."

"For theft. But you've also accused him of murder. And the law of my desert is an eye for an eye." The Sheikh motioned to his servant. "Take him outside."

Feeling dazed, Marcos followed the servant into the courtyard. A dais had been set up at one end and flaming torches lit the darkness of the cooling desert night. An audience made up almost entirely of men sat on rough benches encircling the dais and two empty chairs.

The servant indicated one of the center chairs and left. Aware of the many pairs of eyes affixed to his back, Marcos sat down. He glanced up at the stone walls in time to see Aziz's hard, angry face staring down at him from a window of the second floor.

"I hope you don't mind, old chap, but I thought I'd stay for this."

He turned around to see Sheldon Winter sitting on a bench directly behind him. "What are you doing here?"

Sheldon shrugged. "I came to make sure my sister didn't need my help, but the Sheikh just told me she already left. Now I'm staying to make sure that wife-stealing bastard gets his just deserts." Shaking his head in disgust, he looked at Marcos. "As little as I like you, I'm on your side. At least you had the decency to ruin my company rather than seduce my wife."

Marcos narrowed his eyes. "And you're really giving up the company? Or did you lie to Tamsin about that?"

"No, she can take the whole damn thing. I never wanted to run a women's cosmetics company but I thought I had no choice." Even in the middle of the Moroccan desert, he was wearing slacks and a cardigan as if dressed for the links at St. Andrews' famous golf course. He wiped the sweat and dust off his balding forehead. "It's amazing how liberating it is to fail. At work, at home. I have nothing more to fear. No choice but to start over."

Marcos waved him closer. "Come here, Winter."

"Yeah? Why?"

As soon as he came within range, Marcos punched him in the face.

Sheldon nearly fell over. He straightened, looking furious. "What was that for?"

"For the bruise on Tamsin's cheek two weeks ago."

"Oh." Sheldon rubbed his jaw wryly. "Guess I deserved it, then."

Marcos stared at him, blinking. This was the man he'd focused on for twenty years? This was the enemy whom he'd thought of night and day—this prematurely middle-aged, flabby failure of a man?

He glanced back at the empty window. Aziz was even worse. Violent, cruel and greedy. A thief. A liar.

But not a murderer.

Tamsin was right. Getting vengeance on Aziz today—even the ultimate revenge, death—wouldn't bring him peace. Because the person Marcos really wanted to punish was himself. And, for the last twenty years, he had.

Marcos took a deep breath, remembering his family, remembering the laughter and love, and the day it had all disappeared. But it wasn't Sheldon's fault or even Aziz's. It was Marcos who had destroyed their lives when he'd run away to start a career in revenge.

But he'd only been twelve. Barely more than a kid. And, for twenty years, he'd been paying for that mistake.

Was it possible that he could just let it go? That he could forgive himself for what he'd done?

I'm sorry. Papá, Mamá, Diego. Marcos closed his eyes. *I'm sorry.*

As if in response, he felt a sudden peace rush over him. His heart opened, letting in the light.

And he suddenly knew that Tamsin was right. He had to end the darkness. For his family. For Tamsin. For everyone who'd ever loved him.

At that moment a hush fell over the crowd. Sheikh Mohamed ibn Battuta al-Maghrib and five elderly men crossed the dais. The Sheikh spoke ringing words in Arabic, demanding that his nephew come out to face the charges.

Aziz slowly stalked into the other chair, glaring at Marcos with eyes of hate. Marcos had no doubt that the other man would have loved to tear him apart. But why shouldn't he be angry? Marcos thought. By accusing him of murder, Marcos had lied…

"We will hear the evidence," the Sheikh said.

No, Marcos thought. He had to end this now, get his car and rush back to Agadir before Tamsin's plane left for London. He had to tell her he loved her and take her in his arms.

Her love was a candle in the window, guiding him home after a long, cold night.

"Wait," Marcos said in halting Arabic as he rose to his feet. "Stop the trial." Looking at Aziz, he took a deep breath. "I was wrong."

Go in swinging, Tamsin thought for the twentieth time.

She took a deep breath in the privacy of the executive bathroom. The headquarters of Winter International comprised the top four floors of a skyscraper on Old Broad Street, and from the window in the private bathroom she could see the Thames, Tower Bridge and St. Paul's far below. All of southern London was at her feet.

She'd never been so scared in her life.

In two minutes she'd be going in to speak to the members of the board. She not only had to convince them to keep the company whole, but to trust the reins to a twenty-three-year-old woman whose only fame came from the clothes she'd worn and the men she'd dated.

More than one board member had already hinted that, argan oil deal or not, they still wanted to sell the company off to try to scrounge some last bit of worth out of the failing business. And, since the Winter family only held forty percent of the privately owned company, her only hope of holding it together was to convince them she could lead Winter International into profitability.

If they gave her the chance, she knew that she could do it. Sheldon's leadership had left the company's image sagging. What did he know about women? No one had time for the old two-hour make-up-and-grooming routine any more.

Tamsin knew that modern women had things to do and places to go. They wanted to look good in a hurry. She would propose a new, less expensive line for twenty-somethings, with sparkle and bold color. And a more exclusive line for older women, who had more disposable income and wanted to look sophisticated, ageless, glowing. She'd even thought of a new package for busy young mothers: the signature anti-aging cream, undereye concealer for sleepless nights and smearproof lipstick for kissing toddlers' cheeks.

She would streamline the divisions and return Winter International to profitability, saving the jobs of her employees by keeping her own salary low—just enough to support herself and her sister in a small flat. Tamsin was willing to work 24/7, to work in the office by day and go to parties by night to promote glamour for W.I.'s image.

Her heart wouldn't be in it. She'd left her heart somewhere between Spain and Morocco. But she'd learned you could somehow go on living with a broken heart.

Fortunately, her appearance in the mirror gave no indication of her feelings. She looked calm, even chic, wearing a pale yellow suit and slingback crocodile shoes. Her red hair was pulled back into a sleek chignon and her red lipstick was perfect against her pale skin.

Perhaps, after two sleepless nights, her skin was paler than usual. It had been that long since she'd left Marcos in Morocco. Two days since she'd lost her dreams, her hope and her love.

She wanted to wail whenever she thought of him. A hard lump had lodged itself permanently in her throat.

Since her return, she'd hidden her pain and anguish from her little sister, who was still staying with Nanny Holland until Tamsin could move out of her old flat in Knightsbridge and find a new one she could actually afford. For the past two days, she'd tried to throw herself into her work, to make sure her presentation today would be flawless. But, as she stared at herself in the mirror, grief still gnawed at her.

Had Marcos gone through with the revenge?

Was there still any chance for them?

She wondered constantly if she'd made a mistake. Should she have taken him up on his offer to stay and talk? Should she have fought for him, instead of taking the easy way out?

Perhaps it wasn't too late, she thought suddenly. Bianca, always generous, would certainly loan her the jet. She could go to Marcos and offer to move to Madrid, anything he wanted, if only to be part of his life...

No. Raising her chin, she gave herself a hard look in the mirror. A life based on revenge was no life at all. She'd made the right choice—the responsible choice.

So why did she feel so awful?

Sheldon's former secretary knocked on the bathroom door. "They're ready for you, ma'am."

Still lost in thoughts of Marcos, Tamsin almost told Phyllis to forget the whole thing and cancel the shareholder meeting. Then she clenched her jaw. She had the company's employees to think about—people with families. She had to do this for them. For her sister. For herself.

She could do this.

Squaring her shoulders, she marched out of the bathroom and down the hall to face the firing squad, with nothing more than a Powerpoint presentation and last season's Chloé suit to protect her.

Marcos watched Tamsin as she walked down the steps beneath the tall cantilevered building.

Wearing a Burberry raincoat, she strode forward in

the early October drizzle to hail a black cab. She looked different from when he'd kidnapped her, he thought. She'd become a strong, confident woman, able to stand up for what she wanted.

Maybe she wouldn't want him any more, he thought suddenly. Maybe she'd given up on him. God knew there was a city full of men for her to choose from— better men than he was.

But no one would ever love her like Marcos loved her. He would spend the rest of his life doing whatever it took to make her happy. He would prove it to her. All she needed to do was give him a chance, and he swore she would never regret it.

"Pull forward," he ordered Reyes.

His black limousine pulled smoothly to the curb. Marcos opened his door. She glanced down at the car in annoyance, as it was blocking her view of the street. Then she saw him and her eyes widened.

He climbed out of the car. "I couldn't do it," he said, putting his hand over his heart. "I was a fool—"

With a loud cry, she threw her arms around him. He felt her tears against his cheek, mingling with the rain.

"I was afraid I'd lost you," she whispered, kissing his face over and over. "I was so afraid."

"You? Afraid? Never." He held her close. "I'm sorry, *querida*. You were right. I was really trying to punish myself. But I couldn't go through with it once I realized that I was in love with you—"

"You what?" she gasped, drawing away.

He looked into her eyes. Rain was falling more heavily now, plastering her red hair to her head and causing her mascara to trickle beneath her eyes, and to him she'd never looked more like an angel. "I love you, Tamsin."

"Marcos—"

He kissed her in the rain, then pulled her into the car. "Come. You must be wanting dinner. Where can I take you?"

She looked dazed in the warmth and comfort of the back seat. "What happened? It's been two days. Two days."

Clenching his hands, he shook his head in furious memory at the sandstorm that had made travel impossible. "I am sorry I couldn't get here faster. I could have called, but—" he took a deep breath, "—I was afraid you might tell me not to come."

"Did I hear right?" She drew back, her brow furrowed with amazement. "You really let Aziz go?"

"Yes," he said simply. Although even that hadn't worked out the way he'd expected. He'd barely given up his claims against Aziz before Sheldon had sprung to his feet with his own accusations of the man's thievery. The Sheikh had disinherited his nephew, sending him into exile, and the last he'd heard, Aziz was working at a petrol station and Camilla was a dog-washer in Cairo.

Tears formed in Tamsin's eyes and Marcos was suddenly afraid that he was doing this all wrong. Why was she crying? It wasn't at all the reaction he'd hoped for. He'd planned to take her out to dinner, to woo her with gifts and sweet words, and court her as she deserved.

But what if it was already too late? What if he'd hurt her so badly that she didn't want him any more? After everything, he couldn't lose her now. He couldn't...

"Where shall we go to dinner tonight?" he asked with false heartiness. "Nobu? The Ivy? I've heard they're both quite good."

"I think I'll take you out for a change," she replied, wiping her tears with a tremulous smile. "You're looking at the new CEO of Winter International."

His eyes went wide. "Tamsin!"

"Not a very high-paid CEO, I'm afraid, since the company has a lot of debt and our divisions need to be cut to the bone to become profitable again. But, for you, I'm willing to stretch the budget for a curry."

She leaned over and gave him a kiss far hotter than any Vindaloo. The kiss burned through his body and, just like that, he suddenly knew that everything would be all right.

"I've been craving that all day," she said.

"The curry or the kiss?" he managed.

She gave him a saucy smile. "Both."

"I live to satisfy your cravings," he said, reaching for her again. But she pulled back with a frown.

"But Marcos, what are you doing here?"

"Kissing you," he said, wrapping his arms around her and pulling her close. "So, if you don't mind—"

"You're in London," she insisted. "You said you'd never come to London. You made a vow."

He shrugged. "That was the past. And, as I've learned, some promises were made to be broken." He stroked her cheek, looking tenderly into her eyes. "And some promises last a lifetime. You are my future, Tamsin. You saved me from a life of darkness. We can live in London, Madrid, Kathmandu—wherever you want. Because you are my home." Blinking hard, he looked at her. "A day with you is worth twenty years of night."

She reached up to touch the single tear that had escaped despite his best efforts.

"Marcos," she whispered, looking up at him with eyes full of love.

This time, when he kissed her, she kissed him back with abandon. Within moments, they were peeling off their clothes.

And Reyes, as he pulled away from the curb, tactfully raised the privacy screen, leaving them to their sunshine in the storm.

* * * * *

THOROUGHBRED LEGACY
*The stakes are high when it comes to love,
horse racing, family secrets
and broken promises.*

*A new exciting Harlequin continuity series
coming soon!*
Led by New York Times *bestselling author
Elizabeth Bevarly*
FLIRTING WITH TROUBLE

Here's a preview

THE DOOR CLOSED behind them, throwing them into darkness and leaving them utterly alone. And the next thing Daniel knew, he heard himself saying, "Marnie, I'm sorry about the way things turned out in Del Mar."

She said nothing at first, only strode across the room and stared out the window beside him. Although he couldn't see her well in the darkness—he still hadn't switched on a light...but then, neither had she—he imagined her expression was a little preoccupied, a little anxious, a little confused.

Finally, very softly, she said, "Are you?"

He nodded, then, worried she wouldn't be able to see the gesture, added, "Yeah. I am. I should have said goodbye to you."

"Yes, you should have."

Actually, he thought, there were a lot of things he should have done in Del Mar. He'd had *a lot* riding on the Pacific Classic, and even more on his entry, Little Joe, but after meeting Marnie, the Pacific Classic had been the last thing on Daniel's mind. His loss at Del Mar had pretty much ended his career before it had even begun, and he'd had to start all over again, rebuilding from nothing.

He simply had not then and did not now have room in his life for a woman as potent as Marnie Roberts. He was a horseman first and foremost. From the time he was a schoolboy, he'd known what he wanted to do with his life—be the best possible trainer he could be.

He had to make sure Marnie understood—and he understood, too—why things had ended the way they had eight years ago. He just wished he could find the words to do that. Hell, he wished he could find the *thoughts* to do that.

"You made me forget things, Marnie, things that I really needed to remember. And that scared the hell out of me. Little Joe should have won the Classic. He was by far the best horse entered in that race. But I didn't give him the attention he needed and deserved that week, because all I could think about was you. Hell, when I woke up that morning all I wanted to do was lie there and look at you, and then wake you up and make love to you again. If I hadn't left when I did—the way I did—I might still be lying there in that bed with you, thinking about nothing else."

"And would that be so terrible?" she asked.

"Of course not," he told her. "But that wasn't why I was in Del Mar," he repeated. "I was in Del Mar to win a race. That was my job. And my work was the most important thing to me."

She said nothing for a moment, only studied his face in the darkness as if looking for the answer to a very important question. Finally she asked, "And what's the most important thing to you now, Daniel?"

Wasn't the answer to that obvious? "My work," he answered automatically.

She nodded slowly. "Of course," she said softly. "That is, after all, what you do best."

Her comment, too, puzzled him. She made it sound as if being good at what he did was a bad thing.

She bit her lip thoughtfully, her eyes fixed on his, glimmering in the scant moonlight that was filtering through the window. And damned if Daniel didn't find himself wanting to pull her into his arms and kiss her. But as much as it might have felt as if no time had passed since Del Mar, there were eight years between now and then. And eight years was a long time in the best of circumstances. For Daniel and Marnie, it was virtually a lifetime.

So Daniel turned and started for the door, then halted. He couldn't just walk away and leave things as they were, unsettled. He'd done that eight years ago and regretted it.

"It *was* good to see you again, Marnie," he said softly. And since he was being honest, he added, "I hope we see each other again."

She didn't say anything in response, only stood silhouetted against the window with her arms wrapped around her in a way that made him wonder whether she was doing it because she was cold, or if she just needed something—someone—to hold on to. In either case, Daniel understood. There was an emptiness clinging to him that he suspected would be there for a long time.

* * * * *

THOROUGHBRED LEGACY
coming soon wherever books are sold!

HARLEQUIN *Presents*

What do you look for in a guy?
Charisma. Sex appeal. Confidence.
A body to die for. Well, look no further
this series has men with all this and more!
And now that they've met the women in these novels,
there is one thing on everyone's mind....

NIGHTS *of* PASSION

One night is never enough!

**The guys know what they want
and how they're going to get it!**

Don't miss:

HIS MISTRESS
BY ARRANGEMENT

by

Natalie Anderson

Available June 2008.

*Look out for more Nights of Passion,
coming soon in Harlequin Presents!*

REQUEST YOUR
FREE BOOKS!

HARLEQUIN *Presents*

2 FREE NOVELS
PLUS 2
FREE GIFTS!

PASSION GUARANTEED SEDUCTION

HP

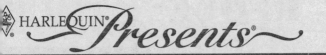

HARLEQUIN *Presents*

Harlequin Presents brings you
a brand-new duet by star author

Sharon Kendrick

THE GREEK BILLIONAIRES' BRIDES

Power, pride and passion—discover how only
the love and passion of two women can reunite
these wealthy, successful brothers,
divided by a bitter rivalry.

Available June 2008:

THE GREEK TYCOON'S
BABY BARGAIN

Available July 2008:

THE GREEK TYCOON'S
CONVENIENT WIFE

HP12736

HARLEQUIN *Presents*

EXTRA

TALL, DARK AND SEXY

The men who never fail—seduction included!

Brooding, successful and arrogant, these men can sweep any female they desire off her feet. But now there's only one woman they want— and they'll use their wealth, power, charm and irresistibly seductive ways to claim her!

Don't miss any of the titles in this exciting collection available June 10, 2008:

Harlequin Presents EXTRA delivers a themed collection every month featuring 4 new titles.